Freedom

Diamondsong

A Concerto in Ten Parts

Part 06:
Freedom

E.D.E. Bell

Atthis Arts
Detroit, Michigan

This book is dedicated to Gwynn, Vance, and Vera

who are confident being themselves

and tell me to be, too.

Preface

Dime's journey and my own have intertwined more than I expected. The beginning was intentionally meta: Dime quit her career just as I quit mine. But that's where it was supposed to end—her plans were derailed, but mine were supposed to continue smoothly. It didn't quite work out that way. Apparently I still had my own cliff to fall over. My own identity to find.

When I started this project, I was in a state of deep exploration—about our values as a shared society and our approaches to progress. If you know me, you know I don't like to offer conclusions; I like to offer ideas. I like people to think for themselves and learn from each other. And I thought *Diamondsong* would be that kind of series: an enjoyable, unique tale, but maybe one that would invoke thought and discussion too.

As the series has gone on, our real-life discourse has grown increasingly tense—more openly disconnected. Less nuanced. More conflated. This is for a whole lot of important reasons, but we still have choices how we engage with each other. Which paths we take. And sometimes it leaves me feeling lost, as a voice.

If you don't know, I deal with disordered anxiety, and I had a triggering incident right before I wrote this volume, as well as Part 07. A friend of mine was expressing how upset he was online and asking for answers, and I, also upset, tried to add some thoughts of comfort and hope, indicating my belief in independent thought, keeping pressure on all leaders, continued dialogue, and compassion—along with recognizing the complexities of a shared society. I was attacked repeatedly by someone with their own reasons to be upset, who, in my view, misrepresented these informal comments as complacency and harm, with no desire to understand my perspective or the experiences that have shaped it. The words were severe and the judgment swift, and onlookers delighted in this calling out, including people who hadn't read what I'd said. Any words in defense were offered privately.

This was compounded by both the stress *of this era* as well as the underlying stress a lot of Gen-Xers have been feeling, and don't feel able to express, of having friends and family who continue to proudly hold ideas we believe to be harmful. And of knowing our own pasts hold ideas we were taught, that we've broken through and now repudiate. And of the implication we're not trying to help when the ways that we do are more tailored to our abilities—and more quiet. We didn't grow up on social media (and had our own pressures) and so, for many of us, our approaches are more direct. Less promoted. We're constantly told by public voices that we're not doing enough. That we're not enough. And then, our anxiety is openly mocked.

Like Dime, it left me feeling less excited about exploring ideas and more just scared to talk. Scared of being around anyone not familiar. Like I should crawl into a cave.

I didn't crawl into a cave; I kept writing, through what was truly an open wound. But the only way I could write something genuine was through my own feelings, and so Dime's journey for these next two volumes is heavily influenced by my own struggles at that time. Despite being scared now to tell this story, I've decided to be open with you—to let Dime's journey be read the way it evolved. I hope that you will enjoy it.

I have deep gratitude to Donnie Martino for his insight on this volume, and especially for his candor. (Donnie: *Thank you.*) Thank you to Catherine Jones Payne and Kelsey Ronan for their guidance and care, and thanks to the team, who stick with me and give me the will to persevere: Meghan Cusack, Camille Gooderham Campbell, Sasha Kasoff Moore, Deborah Reilly, and Maria Judge. I couldn't get by without my friends.

Now, to Dime alone in a forest.

Cheers,

E.D.E. Bell

October 2019

The World of Ada-ji

The Ja-lal: A humanoid species, dwelling in the foothills and plains of Ada-ji, characterized by broad advancements in construction, invention, and health. The Fo-ror call them brutes.

The Fo-ror: A winged humanoid species, dwelling in the forests of Ada-ji, characterized by their natural living and the use of magical powers, known as valence. The Ja-lal call them fairies.

The Ja-lal and Fo-ror are similar in form, with gray skin, but differences between them in composition and culture. Pyr is singular for a Ja-lal or Fo-ror and pyrsi is plural.

The pyrsi of Ada-ji hold many **gender identities**. While this doesn't clarify all aspects of gender, it is polite to introduce oneself with a prefix, indicating the appropriate pronouns:

Fe' indicates a set of feminine identities, using the pronouns she/her/her(s).

Ma' indicates a set of masculine identities, using the pronouns he/him/his.

Ji' indicates a set of spectrum identities, using the pronouns ve/ver/vis.

When gender is unknown, it is polite to refer to a pyr with xe/xem/xyr(s). Any group of pyrsi (plural) would be referred to with they/them/their(s).

A pyr may be generically referred to as **Burge**, short for the more formal Burgess, often for purposes of polite address or getting a stranger's attention. This is similar to the use of Sir or Ma'am on Earth. For those who hold social prejudice based on class, the term implies some sense of status or honor.

Ja-lal and Fo-ror may live up to 50 cycles. Their lives are divided into defined **epochs**, aligning with societal expectations:

Aoch Age 0-9 — Characterized by upbringing, education, and exploration

Bakh Age 10-19 — Centered on building family, performing and completing apprenticeships, and finalizing life plans

Gamh Age 20-29 — Fully immersed in their specialty or role, contributing full-time to society

Dorh Age 30-39 — Respected in leadership and/or advisory roles; it is normal to take some time for self

Eroh Age 40+ — Expected to retire and engage in craft or occasional consulting, through the **life expectancy of around 50 cycles**.

Expectations differ for each culture. For example, while a Ja-lal must develop xyr profession into a career, a Fo-ror's profession and rank are set based on xyr social class and other historical and cultural factors.

A **cycle** on Ada-ji is perhaps up to four times the length of an Earth year. So, our main character, at age 20.5 cycles, has lived more than 80 Earth years but, in relation to her life span, could be considered at the **maturity of her early forties** on Earth.

Each **turn** on Ada-ji, a period of day and then night, is **significantly longer than an Earth day**. As such, pyrsi do not sleep according to light or dark, but instead based on their own needs, lifestyle, profession, and schedule.

The Ja-lal measure time by the periodic sounding of bells; they refer to the resultant time periods with the same term. The Fo-ror are less rigid about time-keeping and refer to the equivalent time period as a span. Each **bell**, or **span**, consists of more than two Earth hours.

Smaller amounts of time are referred to by both cultures as **takes**, which can be thought of as about ten Earth minutes.

In Earth terms, it has been about six weeks since the beginning of our tale.

The Ja-lal and Fo-ror live on separate sides of the Great Cliff. They have not interacted since the ***Great War***, an event most noted for being the **end of the Violence** on Ada-ji.

Synopsis to Here

Just after Dime had left her career working for the Circles, the government of the Ja-lal, three hooded figures burst into her home, determined to take her away. Dime and her spouse, Dayn, ran to escape them.

The intruders were revealed to be Fo-ror, commonly called fairies. These fairies, unseen since the conclusion of the Great War, were feared and loathed by the Ja-lal, who were taught that any contact would cause the Violence to return.

Dime escaped the city and was rescued by a large animal species known as newts, where she befriended a young newt she called Juni. Dime was found there by a fe'pyr familiar with fairies, Ella, who broke the news that Dime was biologically a Fo-ror—one whose wings had been removed.

Later, Ella explained that the magical fairy power of valence did not come from the wings, but from the heart. At her recommendation, Dime traveled to the diamond caves, where she confirmed and practiced her powers. There, she discovered that the Ja-lal also have powers of valence, more internally directed. Dime believes very few Ja-lal are aware of, and thus intentionally shaping, their own powers.

Trying to make sense of these events, Dime traveled between the lands of the fairies, the Heartland, and her own Sol's Reach. She reconnected with friends: Zael, who was said to be dying, Ador, the founder of an advocacy group called the Free Winds, Ador's spouse Batu, and Dime's own family: Dayn, Luja, and Tum. She was surprised to run into Rock, an Intel Agent and former flame who had rushed to her rescue upon learning of Dime's original escape.

She encountered new allies: Volana, a fairy connected to a secret Fo-ror discussion group, the Foundry, Volana's friend Uchitar, who struggles with tzetz-addiction, and Hin, a young assistant Ador has taken under his charge.

Dime met with the leaders of each land. First, High Seat Ferala, who confessed that Dime was part of an old scheme to avenge the horrors of a disease called the curse, which the Fo-ror blamed on the Ja-lal. This scheme, designed by now Third Seat Neimano, was named Project Diamondsong. His plan was to remove the wings from Fo-ror newborns, place them in positions of potential influence amongst the Ja-lal, and then allow them to grow up before activating their loyalties as Fo-ror spies. Later, she met with Sala, the Light, who was resistant to her message of working with the Fo-ror. Dime was upset by this and, while leaving, inadvertently revealed her fairy origins.

Dime was able to locate two other potential victims of Neimano: Kolk and Nafat, both of whom she informed of their history and biology. Later, Rock concluded that a respected medic, Olok, was likely also a victim. Dime learned that Rock, against Dime's wishes, went and talked to Olok, who wanted no involvement.

Dime secretly observed a gathering led by High Seat Ferala and Second Seat Layanie. She was surprised to see Ella in attendance, open in her identity and confronting her own deeply set emotions regarding her late spouse's homeland. Afterward, Dime was stopped by Intinpalo, an officer of a political group, the Risers. Dime and Rock got into an argument, and Rock left abruptly. Frustrated by this and Intinpalo's supremacist language, Dime showed him the net that held the newts back from their natural home as evidence of Fo-ror flaws.

After he left, Dime was unexpectedly joined in the forest by her children, along with two of the newts: Juni and Stern Eyes. Then, Neimano and one of his guards found them, attacking her and the others with valence. Stern Eyes reacted in fear, using her own valence to stop Neimano and his guard. Upset, she ran back to turn herself in to their troop, where Dayn was as well. Hoping to help, Juni, Tum, and Luja soon followed, leaving Dime alone in the forest.

There Dime stands, worried that all peace is ready to crumble.

Ulla
Thynell
W
N
E
S
Ada-Ji

Freedom

I was free; but there was no one to welcome me to the land of freedom.

—Harriet Tubman, c1868

Act 1

Away from Here

Emptiness settled into the forest around her and Dime realized, once again, she was alone. Being around the others had energized her, she now understood. And while she'd always enjoyed her times of solitude, she'd had enough of it these last turns.

As with Dayn, as with her children, even now with Rock and the new friends she'd made—the stride she found them again, they were already out of reach. Or maybe she was. She'd lived in Juni's burrow, then in Ella's tower, then the den, then the hut. A sleep here or a sleep there, on the forest floor or in Volana's generously-offered bed. And here she stood, alone in the deep, chattering forest, still shivering from Neimano's cruel attack.

It was all wearing on her.

Yet, if Dime wanted to avoid such things, she should have hidden and stayed hidden. She hadn't. She'd gone to the city, then again. She'd traveled to the forest, then again. Even her family had stayed hidden a good total of one bell before taking to the waters of the almost mythical Sha to find their scaled, feathered friends.

Even at Ferala's speech—or Seat Layanie's speech, as it had gone—she'd been surrounded by hundreds of pyrsi yet still ended up here, alone in the shadow of the ominous rope net, with even her child asking for space as ve trudged off into the forest. And after what had happened. She was still grappling to understand any of it.

That's right; she'd been here too long. She should go.

While she didn't think Neimano or Ulkanet had looked in any shape to return, it would do no good to stand here, giving them the chance.

As Dime made her way to her chair, the flapping of wings grew from the direction of Pito. With no energy for another confrontation, she strapped in and lifted up, Volana's spare chair still tied awkwardly to one side. The wood of the two chairs clattered in an annoyed manner as she rose above the ground and then moved forward. Away.

It was easy now, the valence. She knew it was her pendant. Her confidence. Overconfidence, even. A touch. But she wasn't dealing with fearmongers and non-believers for the moment. She didn't have to.

She was leaving.

A force tugged at her chair, pulling it backward. *Valence! They're pulling my chair with valence!*

Dime grew annoyed at what seemed like an inappropriate gray area, no, not even a gray area. Pulling a chair was no different than pulling a pyr and that was the Violence. How did she become the only pyr to see how far everyone had gone? Pyrsi needed to stop and gather themselves!

Irritated, she turned and zipped back toward the approaching Fo-ror. In the strides before they realized it, her own valence joined the force of those who tried to slow her, and she accelerated, zooming right through the midst of a large group of gawking fairies.

She wasn't sure exactly with whom she was dealing, but they didn't have a terrible air to them. Illuminated by small, hanging glowstones, they wore normal Fo-ror clothing and held kind faces. Their wings shimmered in the chill forest breeze. She didn't think Intinpalo would have sent them, but she couldn't be sure.

Wide with surprise, their eyes tracked her as she passed through them.

While a moment ago Dime had just wanted to get away, she now stopped to face them, hovering both chairs in mid-air. The fairies fluttered and circled around her, expressions ranging from confusion to shock. The layers of their indigo-hued wings highlighted the lack of her own, yet she kept steady, between them. She knew the power of her pendant now. She no longer feared for herself. And no one else was here. Her children were safe.

"Why do you hinder me?" she asked. "Why don't you ask to talk, like normal pyrsi?"

Each seemed stunned, their wings flapping in place. Finally, a pyr responded, his voice trembling. "We have to stop you. We can't let you bring . . . the Violence. Seat Neimano, we saw him. He was . . . harmed." A buzz grew around her at the truth of the harsh language. "He pointed us this way and said we must find and arrest you, on his behalf. Our Seat. Sha's chosen. He said to follow the unusual valence. We didn't know . . . Ja-lal had valence."

Dime wasn't touching that. And there was a more critical point to clarify, if she wanted any chance of leaving without further incident. "I didn't cause his harm." Dime spoke clearly, letting the truth shine from her eyes. She almost mentioned that Neimano had harmed *her*, but she didn't want to incite nor escalate, nor bring the newts into it.

"Look," Dime implored instead. "Look at you, pulling me back from my path. The Ja-lal aren't bringing the Violence here." She swept her arm around, hoping to make the point without accusing them directly. "You only need to stop. Listen. And think. Let's set down. Let's talk a while." She pointed downward and started to lower herself that way.

And just as she thought someone might listen, that perhaps they could gather on the ground and have a rich conversation in the peace and shelter of the trees, one young pyr darted toward her, his light face full of fear and nobility, the charge of obeying his Seats. Then, not tonight.

Sighing, Dime reached into her diamond and did what the fairy wings could not. She shot upward like a pressure pipe, weaving by all senses through the branches and breaking out of the canopy into the dark night sky. And without further hesitation, she sped away, shielding her eyes from the harsh air that pressed against them, flying back over the top of the Great Cliff and over the plains, toward the old woods.

She considered what rumors would start when they realized the valence she used felt not unusual, but just as their own. Considered its power. She should have worked harder to calm them, directed them to the Foundry, perhaps. She couldn't worry about it anymore. What was done was done.

The leaning silhouette of the hut emerged in the dark clearing. Another wave of emptiness pitted Dime as she approached. These moments of fear and tension always caused a tightness in her blood, and once they passed, she felt drained. Beyond that odd physical sensation, she knew that again, she would be alone. Not only could her family not have made it back so soon, she knew they were not there. She would have sensed them. And so she set down on a pad of brush, unsnapped her belt, and dragged her bag back into the impromptu dwelling, devoid of any real comfort—devoid of the companions who had given it purpose before.

With her melancholy an unpleasant yet heavy blanket, she welcomed the pull of sleep.

Dime felt guilty wandering around the base of the old woods trees, the light of Sol streaming through them in bold stripes, so different than the filtered flickers of the deep Heartland forest.

Guilty because she'd slept too long, been slow to rise, and wandered a while around the brush. Guilty because despite all the trouble now stirred, she wasn't sure she'd made any progress at all. The Violence was escalating on both sides of the cliff, and now with the newts as well. Unrest had grown, and she still had no plans other than to get pyrsi talking, something that could have been done much more artfully, she was sure.

At least she wasn't hiding anymore. Even here, she wasn't hiding, just resting. But she was still running, and avoiding, and evading. Sure, it was all for the purpose of not escalating tension, but at what point was she making the tension worse? At what point should she act more boldly?

A crack of thunder sounded out over Sha, and a rain wafted over the waiting forest. Dime rushed to find her bowl and set it out in the clearest spot she could find. Grateful for the shelter of the hut, she sat inside, watching the rain drip down through the trees, the drops much heavier than she was used to.

Rock's abrupt departure wouldn't leave her mind, and she felt guilty about that too. Rock was a grown pyr, a brilliant pyr. If Rock couldn't engage like one, Dime couldn't always fix it. Yet her absence felt wrong. Not as a couple—those times had simply passed and there was no road left that led to them together. But as a team. Rock was right; there was balance between them. They seemed to cover each other's missteps. Whatever Dime was trying to do—frustrating in itself because "bring pyrsi together to talk" didn't sound like enough even though she was sure it was essential—Rock should be there with her.

She felt that.

Or maybe it was more selfish. Sometimes she knew and sometimes she didn't want to. What she did know is she'd been wandering around this peaceful haven while unrest was boiling over all across Ada-ji. A heavy wave of rain passed over the hut, sending in a mist that reached where Dime sat. By instinct, she ran her fingers over her scalp, finding instead her soft layer of hair.

Before all of this, she'd been happy. She missed being happy. Except, that wasn't true. She'd left her career because of the cross-current in the wind, in her lack of ability to do anything to help. So, now, she could help. In theory.

One pyr trying to make a difference in a big and complicated world seemed to always land a little short. At that thought, she laughed aloud. As petite as she was, she'd only won one jumping contest in her life. And that one just a matter of sheer will against an opponent who didn't really care. She'd still worn the medal like a blessing from the Light.

Well, Dime still cared. She lifted her chin, trying to feel determined or noble, just—anything to boost her spirits. Outside, a bird squawked.

The question was where to go next. She could find Rock. No, she couldn't. Rock wouldn't be found unless she wanted to be, in which case she'd already be here. She could go to the Beds, on the harsh beaches of the Heartland, where Dayn, her children, and Juni were. Except, Luja had asked her to hold back and let them handle it. She could return to Volana's home and offer her any additional help. Or she could return to Lodon. Perhaps try again with Sala.

She glanced at Volana's chair, sitting awkwardly at one side of the shelter next to Tum's wheelchair, which she'd spent some of the early bells cleaning and checking, and her own chair with its bulky storage box and mismatched wood. She really had intended to return the low-backed fairy chair, but after Neimano had sent the crowd to find her, she didn't want to put Volana at risk. So it sat here in the shelter, looking about as confused as Dime as to why.

Then, what else? She could engage the political factions. Volana and her Foundry. Intinpalo and the Risers. Jaza and Sol's Pillars. She cringed at that. Ador and the Free Winds. Batu would know where Ador was, if he wasn't at their home. Or the many less prominent factions, groups or even small clubs whose dialogue and purpose she'd hadn't yet met or explored. Rock probably knew the details on all of them.

Dime sighed. These were all onesie-twosie little moves, and that's all she'd been doing from the first turn of this. Shouldn't she be developing something bigger? Speaking in the plazas of Lodon, similar to how the Seats had called the crowds to their clearing? Trepidation gripped her at the thought. Maybe there was something more.

The rain stopped, and Dime rose, stepping back outside. Unlike the Heartland forest, the water absorbed quickly into the stony ground here, and other than a few puddles, the ground was already almost dry.

She turned and gazed at their little dwelling—the crooked structure of large limbs, leaned together and covered by thatched-leaf panels, and decorated with an evergreen sprig Dayn had stuck by the doorway. The same doorway that had a note still pinned to the inside, letting Dime know where they'd gone.

Water trickled down through the trees and Dime stood, watching each final raindrop hover and plunge from the roof with unpredictable drama. Eventually, she moved back over to the carved bench, swiping the water off with her hands. She sat down, fretting, as the time again passed.

Hearing a rumble and a flurry of cracking brush, she jumped to her feet and whisked behind a wide tree trunk—wide by Sol's Reach standards, she supposed. She peered out, straining to see what approached.

Fear left her quickly, as the light-feathered newt bounded full-up over a rocky ridge with her younger child in her arms.

"Juni!" Tum scolded as they took the landing a little hard. Dime, rattled as any parent would be seeing her child leap an impossible distance in the arms of another youth, hurried toward them both.

"Juni! Tum!"

Neither seemed even a little surprised to see her, as yes, Juni would have smelled her long before now, she thought with a sigh, and probably told Tum she was here. "Hold on," Dime said, turning back to the hut and returning with Tum's chair.

Juni seemed unsure what to do with the wheelchair, but Tum directed her in the newt-like language they'd developed, and Juni sat her onto the ground, dropping Tum's bag next to her with a little less care than Dime would have preferred. Tum opened the sling she wore, and Agni jumped out onto four extended paws, stretching in a long arc before bolting away. Tum ran forward on her arms, pulling herself up into the chair. She beamed back at Juni before giving her mother a furtive glance.

Dime wasn't sure what the glance was for—was something wrong?—then she noticed Juni's nervous stance, her eyes darting about. "Juni?" Dime asked. Panting, Juni dragged to her side, and hesitantly, for they'd long-ago set boundaries on traditional newt greetings, she bent down to rest the top of her feathery head onto Dime's crop of hair.

"Oh, ok, then. Are you well?"

"She's upset," Tum said. "She needs to go back. Let's talk about it then. Just . . . you know, try to make her feel better. She's not going to stay. I told her that was fine. She'll see us again."

Nodding, Dime reached her arm around and stroked the smooth scales that ran down Juni's arm, past her feathers. Juni stood back up, seeming to relax, and Dime noticed the way the feathers around her neck and shoulders had been ruffled, missing many of the little sprigs she liked to wear as adornments.

"Oh, tell her to wait a moment," Dime said, rushing back to a patch of herbs that she'd found. She'd forgotten the name, but Ella used them in teas. Without any juniper close by, they'd need to do. Picking a few robust branches, she returned and held them for Juni to smell.

Juni brightened. Making a growling, gurgling sound, she wriggled the stalks into the top of her feathers. Once they were all placed, she ran her taloned fingers through Dime's growing hair, muttering a commentary Dime hoped was positive.

"She likes it on you, Ma-ma," Tum confirmed.

Dime and Juni's eyes met, and they both, in their own fashion, smiled. Then Juni's expression dampened again. She turned back to Tum.

"Hold on, I know you're leaving." Dime remembered the bowl

she'd set in the rain, and carefully she walked it over to Juni. Juni let a long whine, waving an arm at Tum.

"Aww," Tum said. She clicked, like in question.

The newt chattered.

"She's happy with the stream; she wants . . . me to have it."

Dime carried the bowl to Tum, who did not hesitate in taking a long drink of clean water. Juni grunted in what Dime took as contentment.

After one last exchange of sounds between Tum and the newt, Juni tossed Dime an apologetic tilt of her head and then ran off, climbing back up the ridge almost as quickly as she'd jumped over it, rocks crumbling and scattering in her wake. Tum held the bowl out and Dime carefully took it, taking a drink herself.

She peered at Tum, trying not to think too hard that her middle-grade child was now used to traveling with only a newt companion, or how others might question her parenting at this point. "Have the fairies come to the Beds? Is there . . . any sign the Fo-ror know what happened at the net?" She didn't even want to speak aloud that the newts had valence, but she was sure Tum knew what she meant.

"No, no sign. But the newts are upset." Tum pulled up on her arms. "Stern Eyes ran back and confessed what she'd done before Juni could talk her out of it."

"Oh, no," Dime murmured.

"It's just being honest, Ma-ma. You can't be mad at her for that. But Juni explained it as soon as she and I got back there, and we got everyone to at least settle down. But Stern Eyes, she ran off to find Leader, who I guess lives in a different set of Beds, further sur. So I don't know what's going to happen."

As interested as she was to hear more, she wanted to hear about Dayn and Luja first. Tum would have told her if they were in danger, but she did tend to get distracted by the issues in front of her. "Your father? And Luja?"

"They're coming too. They went the Sha way. I would have gone with them, but Da-da wasn't sure about me climbing back up the ledges."

He could have thought about that before you left.

Tum's face grew stern, as though she'd heard her. "He'd expected all of us to stay there a while, and said maybe you could help us leave when needed. But then he said we couldn't stay after what happened at the net." Tum shrugged, suddenly slumping to one side. "Sorry, I'm tired. Just all the sudden; I didn't think I was before."

"We can talk later, Tum-Tum. Let's get you in and fed, and you can get some rest."

Once she'd helped Tum onto their makeshift bed and sang her a song or two until she was sure the fe'ch'pyr was sound asleep, Dime walked back outside, pacing back and forth, listening for any calls from below. Hearing that Dayn and Luja were well was fine, but traveling Sha's unstable surface on a few floating branches sounded terrifying. There'd be no rest for her until she knew they were well.

She might have flown to search, but then she'd be leaving Tum here alone, and that was simply not happening.

But maybe they were close. As Luja had said back in the Heartland, it wasn't a far distance to Sha from here, just a jagged one, over rugged terrain. She remembered Luja's reassurances to trust Dayn. And she did; it was just . . . she was tired of being apart from him. All her efforts to stay tough had caused her to pack those thoughts away, but now, hoping he and Luja were close, all she could think of was their return.

And soon enough, a sweaty and panting Aoch came lumbering toward her, vis father close in tow. Despite knowing there was no shower here, Dime wasted no time pulling those sweaty pyrsi into her arms. Only once released, did she note the worry in Dayn's eyes.

"She's here," Dime reassured. "She's fine. Agni too—around here somewhere."

Dayn nodded, but the worry did not fully release. "The kids told me about the net," he said, twitching a little. "With Stern Eyes beside herself and then away, we were straining their ability to deliberate more than I was willing to risk. Juni didn't want to agree, but she knew I was right, from what Tum described. She insisted on taking Tum back herself. She's a good friend, you know."

"Yes, she is." Dime noted Dayn's heavy breaths. "Pushed a little too hard back there?" She motioned toward the ledges.

"The rock here is softer; the spikes don't hold. Just took a little creativity, is all." He grinned. "I'm starting to get jealous of those wings."

"I'm not," Luja said. "They'd get in the way, like sleeping and sitting and everything." Ve paused. "I like me just how I am."

Dayn's expression softened, and Dime rested a hand on his arm. "We do too, Buttons."

Luja rolled vis eyes, but didn't look *too* upset at the use of vis old nickname.

"We'll need to catch up," Dayn started. She could see that the idea of their children being attacked by fairy valence was high in his consciousness. But he looked tired, too.

"No, I know. Go get rest." Though Dime had spent bells wandering around aimlessly like a toothcar looking for upcity fares, the fact that her family was here made something feel unstuck, like maybe she could find answers to those questions that had just bounced around. Like everything was right again. Wherever they were, that was the right place.

That had never changed.

She reached her arms out again and locked her spouse in a long embrace.

"I'm glad you're alright," he said. He seemed to have more to say, but instead shook his head.

"Yeah," Dime said, feeling equally worn. "It's a lot. Go ahead," she added, pointing toward the hut. Suddenly, she wasn't eager to wander around the woods alone again, but she did have an idea. "While you sleep, I'm going to go see if Ella's back yet, if that's fine." She hesitated, then the words rushed out. "Don't leave?"

"We'll be here," Dayn said with a tired smile.

Dime had been at Ella's tower at least a bell, and though it had to be at the front of her mind, Ella still hadn't made any mention of her visit to the Heartland. Dime wasn't sure how to broach the topic, or even if she should. So instead, they took a walk outside and Ella taught Dime about various plants unique to the old woods.

"And Friend," Dime asked. "What variety is Friend?" It would be rude to ask a biological question about any member of a homegroup, but as they'd just walked around pointing at and labeling plants of every color and shape, certainly the topic wasn't so far out of range.

"Not really sure. Friend was found by Suzanne, deep outforest—almost as far as the delta, long even before I met her. They are very sensitive plants, you could say. They tend to disappear anywhere the Fo-ror move in, nor do they care for the newts. Besides being reclusive, the Fo-ror haven't found any use for them, so I'm not sure they even have a name. Anyway, Suzanne found Friend nestled behind a felled tree on the edge of a remote village, one newly built by the sort that liked to stay away from the city. She saw its needles curling, and she believed it wasn't going to survive there—and so she asked it if she could take it home."

"She asked?"

"Oh, who knows. That's what she said. And how can I argue; you should have seen it when she died." Ella pulled her lips together a moment. "Knowing what Suzanne would have asked me to do, I sat by it over the course of turns, talking to it. Letting it know I didn't have anyone else, and I'd be honored if we could be there for each other." Ella again drew a tight expression, and Dime considered whether she was embarrassed for saying she'd sat and talked with a plant. Dime hoped she wasn't.

As if coming to that conclusion herself, Ella lifted her chin.

"Friend has been just that for me a very long time. I suspect it's old, too. Maybe older than any of us."

As they walked in silence a while, Dime considered whether she should interrupt Ella's peace here by telling her about the newts. Though, she felt, Ella had answered that question herself with what she'd done in Pito. Or maybe, when she'd gone the first time to look for Dime. No, she had to know.

"We ought to talk about the newts."

Ella stopped in place, her eyes narrowing. "I'll make some brew," she said, turning back toward the tower. Dime followed her in through the smooth, carved door and up the winding staircase, dotted with tiny, colored glass windows that streamed in the light.

And, unsure why, but feeling in her heart that this cozy room was home, Dime sat on the second floor of Ella's tower, seated with the older fe'pyr at the thick wooden table, and inhaling the rich, soil-evoking scents of properly made brew. She allowed a moment of warmth knowing, no matter how difficult her news would be, this was one place she didn't have to worry about just saying it. So she did.

"Third Seat Neimano and one of his guards followed me after the event. I bet he was there the whole time, skulking around in the crowd somewhere. I had already been followed by someone ranking in the Risers, and I'd been using valence, so it wasn't a difficult trail to follow." Dime caught her breath. Ella waited.

Dime had said this was about the newts so Ella likely knew there must be more. She continued on. "The issue was, by the time he found me, I'd run into Juni, Tum, Luja, and Stern Eyes out by the newt net. I know," she waved a hand. "That sounds sort of random. Well, I suppose I didn't run into them; Juni smelled me and they came to where I was."

Ella nodded at the correction, but again waited.

"Ok." Dime needed to back up. "Before leaving for the Heartland, I'd hidden my family to keep them safe, not too far from here, and the moment I left, they left too. Not so interested in safe, apparently.

They went to the Beds." Ella sat up at this. "The kids had shown the newts how to dig under the net and make a passage, and Juni was running around with them doing it. So they were on the inside of the net, checking things out. I don't know. They're all young, right? Except Stern Eyes, of course. She caught up to them just after I did and didn't seem to approve, as she was giving them much the same eye I was."

"But Neimano showed up," Ella prompted.

"Yes, and his guard. Ulkanet, I believe. Don't know xyr pronoun. Neimano, well," there was no need to hide the truth here, she reminded herself, "he . . . attacked us."

Ella's eyes widened.

"Right. Not even grabbed-my-arm or pushed-me attack, but something—" Dime didn't want to describe the sensation of her breath constricted and her limbs tight. She couldn't forget the feeling, but she didn't want to describe it. So she moved on, trying to steady her shaking voice.

"You probably even know about this, but either way, well, Stern Eyes attacked them back. Also with valence. Newt valence. It was like a bolt of lightning in a storm, made solely of her anger. I mean, she was afraid for us, but the fear became anger? She stunned them both. Neimano staggered away, but Ulkanet was left unconscious. Luja, my dear Luja, refused to leave xem, and spent time we could have taken to get away from the situation tending Ulkanet, until xe too flew off.

"Stern Eyes had already left in a panic; we sent Juni and Tum back to try and find her. According to Dayn—well, they're all back in the hiding place now—Stern Eyes confessed to the troop what she'd done and went off to find someone Tum calls *Leader*. Dayn didn't want to exacerbate the tension or hinder their discussions, so he returned with the kids to the old woods. Juni carried Tum back there, but she was clearly distressed, leaving as soon as she'd arrived. We think Neimano thinks I'm the one that attacked him, using my diamond. But we can't be sure."

"Oh, dear." Ella walked to the cabinet and pulled out two shot glasses and a bottle. Dime noted with some amusement it was *not* the gold-set bottle from Pito. Nevertheless, she did not hesitate in mirroring Ella as the Dorh knocked the liquid back.

"I should have realized," Ella said, pausing before shrugging and pouring herself a second shot. "Something one of their elders told me once, a long time ago. Made it sound like they were familiar with the diamond caves. As soon as he mentioned it, he cut himself off, and rephrased it to say that the newts knew all of the land's cracks. Then he didn't like that, and changed it again to say something that felt unrelated. I asked him again about the diamonds, and he acted like he didn't know what I meant. I made a note in my journal—"

Ella stared at the wall. "If we could only let them be," she said, mostly to herself. "What about you? What are you feeling right now? Not just the newts," she waved a hand, "but all of it."

"I'm confused," Dime answered. "And tired. And feeling like I'm just bopping around doing the same things and not changing anything. Like, I have these great friends, but there are so few of us compared to all of Ada-ji, and how are we going to build what we need to build from scratch in the time we may have to do it?"

Ella chuckled.

Dime didn't see what was funny about that.

"So that's the thing," Ella started, at least tilting her head to offer some slight apology for laughing. "What you're saying is what they've taught you."

"I don't follow," Dime said.

"That's what they want you to think. That it's insurmountable." She rested her hand on the table, before lifting it. "The way the world works," Ella continued, "the system is designed to push back anyone who steps forward alone." She flicked her fingers. "Right back into place, you go!" She lowered her hand again.

"It's never that blatant; it just feels that way. It's more like, a pyr steps forward, and the air is too thin, and xe either steps back or eventually xe loses xyr voice or withers away in the silence. That's how oppression works.

"We don't talk about the Great War anymore, because life moves forward either way, and the Circles keep pre-war texts out of view. But I've found a few over the cycles. Believe it or not, Ada-ji was not always even so kind. The problems we see now are only shadows of the strife that our ancestors endured and overcame.

"And though issues are more specific now, such as class structure and hemsa, they are no less important. Our steps forward grow more refined, but they are still steps we all must push to take." Ella returned to her brew, taking a sip. "Those who resist these advancements offer us an illusion. They offer the idea that one pyr must step forward alone. It's a myth! We are not alone. We never were. And if we let that illusion permeate our thought, then the brave few suffer and the shadows return. Before we even notice them."

Dime considered this—how many pyrsi were out there who might already be open to new ideas. And how one could energize such a group of pyrsi, when those in power insisted those pyrsi didn't exist. That they were a minority. A niche. She wondered if Ella was right.

"There is a place," Ella said, hesitation slowing her words. "A place called the Underground." The last words were whispered; Dime almost couldn't hear them.

This had come out of nowhere, which likely meant Ella had been considering it for a while. She knew the feeling. "The Underground?" Dime tried to confirm.

Ella grimaced. "Look, we don't talk about it. I decided you needed to know, and I stand by it. Still, stop saying the name." Ella glanced around, as if Sala were listening in the stairwell. "Do you have that map on you?"

The map that Beb had given her back in Lodon was tucked into her backpack, inside the hut. Not far from here, but not on her. "No. But I could go get it."

"No, it's fine. Since you can fly, it's easy anyway." Ella took a take or so to draw a crude map on a sheet of paper. Dime tried not to peer too far over as she sat, entranced by the scratching of the pencil. "Promise me you'll destroy this once you've learned it." Dime nodded. "Anyway, it should be cryptic enough without context." Ella pointed, walking her through what each of the symbols meant. She stopped and described the landscape in detail, holding her gaze against Dime's as if to emphasize she would only hear this once.

"Got it?"

"Yes, I think so," Dime said.

"No, not think so! Do you know how to get there or not?"

"Yes, I— Yes, I know how to get there." She closed her eyes a moment, memorizing those last details, the way she had after her meeting with Ferala.

"Good." Ella sat back in her chair, as if that was it.

"So what is it again? You've told me nothing."

"What part of secrets is confusing to an IC agent? Think of it as one of your dens, but much more serious. I'm not telling you more."

"Ok, fine. But—you said pyrsi live there? In this den?"

Ella raised an eyebrow. "Yes, since sending you to an abandoned ruin to kindle a movement wouldn't be much fun, then yes. Pyrsi live there." She folded her hands over her lap. "Suzanne and I could have lived there. We discussed it, even argued over it, sometimes taking opposite sides of the debate than we had the turn before. It's a nice place, beautiful even." Her gaze reached away from the tower now, distant, and Dime wondered what she was seeing. "But it is also an illusion. An admission of failure, the way she and I both saw it. I would rather live here, suffering the wind, than sheltered from it. But, that's just me. I suppose I'm not like most pyrsi."

"You're definitely not," Dime agreed, her mind racing with what this place—where this place—could be. Ella had really mentioned it out of nowhere. Dime gazed at the fe'pyr. "Have I told you how much I admire you?" She was still thinking of her appearance at Pito, but since Ella hadn't brought it up, Dime didn't feel she should.

"No. You haven't. But thank you." Ella sipped from her mug, a slight gleam to her eyes. "Just . . . be careful. It's the sort of place that pyrsi are absorbed into. Everyone who goes there has a reason, and then those reasons begin to consume them. Soon, they're isolated from the pyrsi they left at home, and then they begin to justify that isolation— Now, look, I've said enough. The point is, we knew we couldn't stay. They don't even like to let pyrsi leave, but it's not as if they would stop you, really. We softened it by suggesting we needed time to gather our thoughts."

Ella laughed. "It wasn't untrue. I'm just still gathering them." She sighed. "We had a good life here. I don't regret it, or maybe I can't." Her eyes cut over to Dime. "I just need you to trust me. I can't go there myself. I just . . . can't. You'll be fine. You won't be alone there, and you're strong enough to know when and how to leave. Your family will love it, oh, how your children will be in their element. And Dayn too, more than you'd realize. *Heh.* Where wouldn't Dayn fit in." She shook her head. "That's one caketop of a spouse you found yourself. I hope you know that."

"Of course I know that."

"Anyway, someone you know is there; you won't even feel alone." Ella winced. "I'm saying too much. You do this to me! You just need to trust me and go. Do you think I'd lead you astray? Besides, didn't you come here all asking where to go? Well, I'm telling you. That's the place. Worth a visit."

"Wait." Dime was really curious now. "Who is there that I know?" She wondered if it was Ador. He'd seemed to know about the Crossing, and Batu had talked about wanting to visit the Heartland. Dime knew she was being rude, but Ella was being so cryptic, and it wasn't like Ella could actually be coerced.

"Former Agent Diamond. This is not how it works; there are strict rules and for very good reason, at least until you waltz in there and turn the place upside down. Which I expect. But I really think it could be good for you in several ways. First, you need a break, and this place is perfect for that, removed from reality as much as it can be. Second, it'll convince you that you're not alone.

You're not starting from scratch. You just need to find the pyrsi who agree with you, and convince them it's time to act. The power hanging over your heart isn't nearly as potent as the power of open hearts all around."

"But just say who's there." Dime tried again. "No one is anywhere near here. Come on, it's just us. I'm going to find out anyway." Dime understood secrets and caution, but Ella's tower stood quite alone.

Ella glared. "No! No one tells. And I'm not saying another word." She tapped the mug on the table. "I've already said way more than I should, but I'm sure they'd all agree you are a most unique case." Ella chuckled. "That hair. Even there, you'll stand out with that hair." Dime thought she was referring to the length. The fairies grew their hair long, and Dime's was still a short, white crop. "I do love it, by the way."

Well that was fine. For changing the subject. "You're being more than frustrating, you know."

"Sure. And I've already broken the hungrypyr's share of their rules so you can stop whining about it and just get there and see for yourself. If your family is out there sleeping on leaf-mats, I assure you they won't protest."

"Alright," Dime said, feeling most unsettled by all the mystery of this unspoken place. Yet, Ella wouldn't send her somewhere inherently unsafe. And her family wasn't going to stay waiting in that hut, anyway. She saw how long they'd stayed there the last time. This was as good a plan as any. Well, then, to the Underground. She sighed, and Ella seemed to relax, noting Dime's unspoken acquiescence. "*Uhh*," Dime pouted. "But, one thing? Could I borrow your shower first?"

Within a bell, clean, lightly perfumed, and with a new batch of Ella's roasted brew beans in the back of her chair, Dime flew back to the hut. She was glad to see that the old woods, even with its pokey-topped trees, hid any signs of their shelter from above. Just in case Neimano's guards were looking out this way. She landed and left her chair behind the hut, following a rhythmic scratchy noise.

Dayn was using a forked stick to clear a homey little path that wound around the side of the impromptu shelter. "I know we're not staying here," he said, without looking up. "But I can only sit and mull for so long. As my mother always says."

Dime smiled. Dayn was close to his parents, as she was to her father. Before they'd left the city, she knew he'd managed to get a sealed letter off to his brother, Coba, who'd left the city long ago to pursue a mining career to the norwes. She didn't know what Dayn had written, and she hadn't asked, but she figured it had to do with reassuring his parents he and the kids were fine, in case they heard anything. He'd mentioned sending an update from the village, the one by the sur den. Probably to let Coba know Dime was well too, but it would be a while before they'd be by.

She'd offered to check in on his parents, but Dayn said they were better off not knowing for now. They'd moved outgate, not even really Nor Lodon, but halfway between the city and the foothills village where Coba and his family lived. They didn't get out too much, and they were probably oblivious to the news.

Speaking of which, Dime figured she might as well get to it. "So, on that note, I'd like to go . . . somewhere new."

He stopped and stood straight, letting the stick fall to the side. "How new?"

She lowered her voice. "Ever heard of an Underground? I mean, not your Boring Project or normal caves. A place *called* the Underground."

He shook his head, as Luja and Tum popped around the side, Luja walking and Tum wheeling to where they stood.

"Hey, loves," Dime said, throwing them each a little grin. "Apparently there is a secret place where pyrsi live and we're not allowed to know anything about it until we go there."

"I'm in," Luja said.

Dime couldn't help but laugh.

"I mean, it has beds and showers, I'm assuming? It's . . . reputable?" Luja raised vis hands in question.

"I don't know. It might just be a bunch of pyrsi sleeping out on the plains."

"Ma-ma," Tum interrupted. "We aren't staying here."

Dayn chuckled with her. "We do have a little pact going on that issue. So if you've got a place, we'll try it?" He turned to their children. "Who's up for more adventure?"

"We are!" They called in unison, arms raised into the air. As if on cue, Agni leapt through the air with a vibrating coo, landing in the center of all of them. Her scruffy tail swished to one side and then the other.

"Ok, that's four yes votes. I suppose I'm in then as well." Dime had to admit, she trusted Ella's judgement and her curiosity was now fully piqued.

"It has to be Ja-lal and Fo-ror living together, right?" Luja's hands were against vis sides. "Sounds underground to me."

"That was my presumption, especially when Ella mentioned she and Suzanne had discussed going there." Suddenly Dime felt uncomfortable talking about it here in the open, even if the open was a secluded place where literally no pyr lived. But she didn't want to betray Ella's trust—or endanger the pyrsi they might meet. She lowered her voice. "They are together at the Crossing also." Dime had only been through what she'd later learned was a rather infamous cliff passage once, with Ella. The other times, she'd either scaled the cliff closer to Pito, or later, flown across it.

"But the Crossing really isn't a 'living' place; it's more like a . . . hangout. A trading post, without any hint of comfort." She recalled the dusty path and the closed-feeling tents and shacks. "This sounds different. More like a place pyrsi stay long-term. So hopefully it's nicer. Ella suggested you'd like it."

"Wow," Luja said. "Back up a step. You're already at whether this co-fairy place is more jazz than the last co-fairy place. You know, the rest of us haven't even been around the fairies. We met Uchitar and Volana, but we didn't see how they live. And of course, I saw the two, you know, but—" Luja didn't seem to know how to describe their encounter with Neimano, and Dime couldn't blame ver. "I mean, let's just go."

Dime took a breath to realize Luja was absolutely right. She hadn't considered that even though she hadn't seen much, she'd eaten and slept in a fairy home. She'd visited their government. Their sacred caves! She'd sat through a huge public event. And here she was casually assessing a joint Ja-lal Fo-ror town. If that's what it was, though she suspected Luja was right about that.

"Yes, sorry, that's a good point. Well, does anyone need more time here?"

They all shook their heads. "Ok, then. I won't say the specifics, but since you'll be with me and see where we're going, wherever we're going is apparently on the other side of Ada-ji from the Crossing. Far sur and eas, by the Great Cliff." She didn't want to say this last part, but it sounded like they'd be traveling *into* the ravine.

Even farther out than the outer reaches of the surcity corridor, the remote corner of Sol's Reach was much like all of the sur plains: too close to the Great Cliff for safety, comfort, and staying on the right side of the Circles. Any villages were scattered and small. And as the far reaches of the sureas plains were even rockier and less navigable than those to the surwes, and as she now knew, the Great Cliff was even higher, Dime figured they stayed mostly untraveled.

As such, she could not imagine a large gathering there. Agents did deploy along the sur border on occasional assignments, if just to check on the small towns that did dot the far reaches. Any secret village would have been reported.

Dime recalled, with discomfort, Ella had called it the Underground, which did have a literal flair to it. Yet any gathering couldn't be within the ravine; it would be much too dangerous when waters flooded down from the mountains. But, perhaps, there was a hidden ledge, or a small cave, like one of the dens. The Crossing wasn't really so large, side-to-side, and Dime hadn't known that existed either.

Though, she was certain the IC did. Someone did. So, then,

did they know about the Underground as well? Or was this truly hidden?

"Ma-ma?" Tum wheeled forward to tap Dime's arm.

"*Hmm?*" Dime looked down.

"You're staring at the tree. Should we, you know, go?"

Dime laughed. "Everyone agrees, right? Last chance to object."

"It's better than this?" Luja deadpanned, pointing vis hand back at their hand-constructed, unpopular dwelling.

"It's a nice hut," Dime defended. No one responded except perhaps Tum, who yawned. "Well, then, we'll go check out . . . this place."

Dayn raised his eyebrows.

"Look, she said it was a secret. Let's just go there, and we'll have more to say about it there. Alright?"

"Sure, it can't get weirder." Luja glanced around. "So what's the flying plan this time? I didn't love the teetering chairs."

That was a good point. She gazed over at the hut and at the beautifully woven roof panels Tum had helped make. "Are we coming back here?"

"No," the others said in unison. Dime almost thought she heard Agni's squeak in there. "Well."

With a swing of her arm, she ripped off two of the roof panels on one side of the structure, lowering them to the ground. Next to them, she pulled off several sections of frame, laying them out in the rough shape of a tiny deck, not a stone deck as she was used to, but wooden like she'd seen in Pito. The exposed branches of the roof structure came off next, to build a low railing around the edge.

For the next bell, they reinforced the structure, Dime taking the last loose nails from her backpack to ensure it was sturdy and stable. "Welcome to my toothlesscar," she said. No one laughed. Getting a nod from Tum, she used valence to lift her, chair and all, and set her down onto the center. The others stepped in and sat down, taking their bags with them. Dime's backpack bulged again, heavy with all her supplies and Rock's carved owl. She'd have a home for it someday, she promised herself.

Hesitating, Dime realized she might want access to her chair. She almost asked the others, but then realized she was the one who'd have to lift it anyway. She stopped to look at Volana's extra chair, but it was still sheltered by what remained of the roof. She'd get it back to Pito eventually. Holding her hand forward, she guided her own chair back onto one corner of the platform, then went to join the group. Wanting to be able to see where she was going, she remained standing, steadying herself against the chair's storage box.

If Dime should have considered the difficulty of lifting four pyrsi, four bags, two chairs, a kita, and a bulky treebranch deck all while standing upright without a secured handhold, she did not. Yet her valence, amplified through her diamond pendant, handled it easily, as the platform rose steadily above the spindly woods. She could see Ella and Friend's tower in the distance as they turned sureas, but she would not put Ella at further risk by bringing this much valence her way. She could sense valence herself, now, and she didn't feel anyone near them, but there was no sense in being irresponsible.

She wished she could have flown lower as they moved across Sol's Reach, but she couldn't have someone looking up and being spooked by the huge flying rectangle. And so they enjoyed the plains from high up, marveling at how tiny each hill and village looked from so far above.

"Is this how the Fo-ror see us?" Luja asked, leaning over a little father than Dime was comfortable. She resisted the urge to pull ver back.

"No." It wasn't. She remembered earlier conversations with Uchitar. "The Fo-ror only fly as high as they have to, and they land frequently to rest a stride. Flying higher just tires them more, and it's more dangerous, in case they have an issue. Flying with wings seems a lot more like running—as opposed to moving an object like I do, which relies only on the use of valence."

"Does anyone do that?" Tum asked. "Fly with an object?"

"I haven't seen it." Dime remembered Ella's friendly chastising that just because one hadn't seen a thing done before didn't mean it hadn't been. Usually the opposite. "Probably at some point. But not normally."

The group stayed mostly quiet as they traveled, absorbing the beauty of Sol's Reach from above, the Great Cliff lingering off to their right in the distance. Finally, she could see the land cut in two by the ravine, no longer a massive canyon like outside of Lodon, but still a deep gouge in the land.

Not wanting to take strong valence too close to their destination, she circled around a few times. Spotting a section that looked flat enough, she set down in between a set of tall crags. Hopefully the platform would stay hidden here. She stood a moment, memorizing the shape of the jagged pillars around them so she could find the place again.

Dime lifted Tum off of the platform, and Dayn moved behind her, taking the back-facing handles of her chair. Turning to Dime, he gave her a look she understood. He wanted to push her himself. No unexpected valence. Dime nodded, and Dayn hesitated.

Whispering something to Tum, he left and walked over to Dime. "It's good to be with you," he said, leaning in with a brush of his lips to her face.

"We'll get through this," she said. "I'll make sure."

"I know," he replied, going back to push Tum's chair as Luja trudged on ahead. The walk to the ravine felt as long as the flight had been from the old woods—the faint outlines of mountains over the ravines seemed to never grow larger as they walked in their direction. Feeling the warmth of Sol on her face, Dime couldn't help but think of what her father had always said about Sol's guidance— to trust where Sol leads. She'd tried to, in her own way.

Dime kept an eye out for the markers Ella had described. She grew worried as the ravine loomed before them and she still had no idea where they were supposed to descend. "We should be close," she muttered.

"Close?" Dayn replied. "We're at the end."

He had a point. With the ravine in front and the Great Cliff not really so far to their right, there wasn't anywhere else to go. Dime gazed around.

"It's hidden, right?" Luja offered. "So if you're going the way Ella said, maybe we just need to go as far as we can." And so they did, walking on until the ridge was just a jump away. Dime glanced protectively at her children, but Dayn held Tum's chair tight, and Luja stayed near him. Furtively, she stepped toward the edge. Feeling nervous, she sat down and scooched forward, until finally she could get a view into the ravine.

Certainly not as ominous as the vast depths near the city or the Great Cliff nearby, the rock fell away to a ledge of smooth, worn stone, then dropped off again. Either way, there was no secret village in sight. Across the ravine, she saw the low peak that Ella had described, and the raised crag in front. This was supposed to be it. She could see another flat patch just past. "It's smooth over there too," she pointed, calling back to Dayn. "Maybe we try that way?"

Dime moved backward, slowly rising to a stand. As Dayn turned Tum's chair, a deep voice called out. "Um, who's there? Please announce yourselves."

She jumped, and her eyes met Dayn's in alarm. But it was a friendly voice. She took a breath. The way the voice had echoed in the ravine, Dime wasn't even sure which direction she should be responding. "Yes, hi, we're looking for the Underground," she called back, unsure if she could be heard.

The voice took a while to respond. "Is your sponsor here?"

"Sorry, I don't know what a sponsor is, but someone told me to come to this place." Remembering Ella's words, Dime had a sudden sense she should be direct. "I was told it wasn't quite the rules, but that you'd find me a unique case."

The voice paused. "Who are you, special case?"

She looked back to Dayn. He nodded. "I'm Fe'Diamond. I was uh—" She considered how much to say, or how to explain this part.

A clanking sound interrupted her fretting, from a stretch down the ravine. A gear and chain device had emerged from the side of the rock, somewhat like a tower bucketpull, but large and made of metal. The chain turned and a pyr came into view, rising toward them on a small metal platform. Luja gasped beside her, and she squinted to see what caused vis reaction.

A pyr living in the ravine was plenty to consider, but this pyr had something Dime had never seen in her life. Hair growing out of xyr *chin.* Dime had never had to worry about shaving her chin, but many, often ma'pyrsi, did do it, including Dayn. They didn't just do it, they did it by the bells, just as they shaved their scalp and brows.

Beyond that, xyr chin hair had been partially dyed a vibrant blue, highlighting the brightness of xyr eyes. Xyr scalp was densely tattooed, with everything from comic characters to patterns to commemorative marks. Xe had no wings, and wore an almost sheer tunic over a colorful, sleeveless top and dark pants. The tattoos, continuing down xyr arms, were visible through the puffshroom-tinted sleeves.

The pyr had hopped off the platform to the top of the ravine and was walking their way. "Well, let's go say hello," Dime murmured, and they moved as a group to meet xem, Dime ushering them all just a little farther from the edge.

"Ji'Bown," ve greeted, once they reached ver. "I've heard of you; I admit it. Now, tell me more about this 'unique case,' if you would."

Dime looked at the ji'pyr with a fascination she was trying to place. It wasn't just the facial hair, or the bright colors, or the fact that ve'd ridden a . . . chain-pull to the top of a ravine at the unoccupied edge of Ada-ji. Ve had an air of openness that drew her in. That hair and blouse and comic characters and everything else—this pyr was strictly verself. Yet, ve looked very nervous. Dime wanted to set ver at ease.

"I will," she promised. "I really am the pyr you heard about. And I know it's a secret here, so I don't want you to worry. Please. Tell me. What is this place?"

Their eyes locked together.

"This place is freedom, Diamond," ve replied. "But only for those ready for it."

She thought only a stride. "Call me Dime. Also, I'm a Ja-lal who is biologically a Fo-ror. No wings, though." She threw her fist back, thumb pointing over her shoulder. "That's why they came for me."

The weight of a thousand towers left her chest as she said the words, with the light of Sol streaming down onto her face and her family tight at her side.

The pyr stood, stunned, and then vis face broke into a broad smile. "Welcome home, Dime. And your friends?"

"Oh, yes, sorry." She turned around. "This is my spouse, Ma'Dayn. He puts up with me and I really like him."

Dayn rolled his eyes but couldn't hide a grin. He nodded at Bown.

"These are my children, Ji'Luja and Fe'Tum." She pointed in turn. "They are all Ja-lal, the way we traditionally see it, but they are open to a world of Ada-ji. I need to tell you, before I go in. I am trying to spread that message. To those who would listen."

Bown looked uneasy. "There are rules, here. If you go in, well, pyrsi don't usually leave. But I don't want to turn you away either. I don't think that I can. If you go in . . . I must have a pledge of your silence. Forever. No matter how things go: this place can never be mentioned outside its boundaries. Our existence relies on the lack of knowledge we exist." Ve rubbed vis scalp.

"We promise," Dayn answered, with Tum and Luja murmuring their assent.

Dime wanted to think through that more, but the others' quick response didn't allow for much pause. And it did seem they'd given the pyr quite a fright. *All in.* "I promise as well. I'll be open with my thoughts, but any choice is yours alone."

Bown nodded. "Let's get out of view, then. We've been out here far too long as it is. Luckily, I'm in charge, you could say, so the rules are at my discretion anyway."

Dime took the hint of warning in that as much as she did the welcome.

As it turned out, the platform Bown had used was built for three pyrsi, and easily fit Tum's chair. Dayn took Tum first, and when Bown returned, ve escorted Luja and Dime onto the platform.

Dime couldn't miss that Luja's eyes shone with excitement. She was glad. "I wonder what it's like," she said. Luja only nodded.

With the chain clanking loudly beside them, they lowered in through a passage in the stone. Stepping off of the platform, they waited as Bown operated a second lever, sliding the chain device back into a carved space in the side of the cliff, hidden from view.

Together, the five pyrsi walked through a stone door, which boomed shut behind them. A small stone table held spiced candles in a curved recess of the stone wall, enveloping the entrance in a warm glow. A hallway stretched before them, lit by glowing fairy stones in regular intervals. From the distance, sounds of conversation wafted toward them, only a soft murmur from where they stood. Only then did Dime remember Agni, who Dime was glad to see was bouncing excitedly in Tum's arms. The kita offered a tiny squeak.

"Welcome to the Underground," Bown said with a slight bow. "Now, let's find you a room?"

Interlude

Pushing through the open burrow felt a little like dying. She didn't know what dying felt like, but it was not right to push your face into a place where there was no breath, even if the others said there was food on the other side.

Trying to hold back how scared she felt, she thrust her claws up through the opening, feeling soft greens. She pulled with all her might, and then pushed with her legs to pop out of the open burrow into the fresh air.

She glanced around and saw that she truly was on the forest side of the net. This was exciting, even though she was scared. The flying two-legs were on this side, and they did not want the troop to come in. But the troop was hungry and there was food here. It was bad not to share what was everyone's.

Cautiously, she lowered to all her limbs and crept through the trees, sniffing as she went. She smelled no flying two-legs now, so that was good. But still she was scared.

She had heard what had happened.

Their troop leader, who had a very long and good name, had used the forbidden power to stop the flying two-legs. This same leader who had told them they could never do this! What did that say, when the leader could do things she had forbidden! She grunted, then stopped, for she should not be loud here, on the inside of the bad net.

She had power too. She had all the feelings. Sad and mad and hungry. And if the two-legs—flying or not—could take away their home and their forest, then why couldn't she use the power to stop them?

She was thinking bad thoughts, and she needed to stop. The important reason to be here was to get food. Sniffing the air, she caught a whiff of a very ripe clove patch. Delighted, she bounded toward it.

As she was digging the cloves from the soft soil, soft and brown, not like the rough sand she was used to, their leader came back into her mind. Sometimes when thoughts go to your mind, they are a visitor that cannot be told to leave! She liked their leader, and trusted her. Before this. Now, she did not know what to think. Was their leader bad, for using the power she had said not to use?

Or was their leader right?

She should not be thinking this.

It was not her decision to make. Their leader had gone to see the home leader, and this leader would make that decision. She would stay here, not think about confusing things anymore, and get some cloves to jam into her mouth until there was clove juice in her feathers. Then she would take as many as she could back to the troop.

Oh, and then that open burrow. She did not want to think about that either.

For the moment, she enjoyed the juicy cloves.

Act 2

Underground

Just as Dime resolved not to act surprised by anything they might encounter here, she drew a raspy breath and almost walked right into Luja. Luja offered vis arm out to steady her, yet stood, similarly stunned.

"Are you seeing this?" Tum said. No one answered, though she thought she heard Dayn *heh*.

The tunnel had taken another uphill stretch and opened out into a large room. This space was not lit by fairy glowstones, but by the filtered light of Sol, streaming in through a wide, open wall, like a massive window without panes of glass. She had no idea how far the opening stretched; the room they were in ended on both sides with tall, translucent screens, which appeared to be movable.

When they'd stopped a take ago, standing atop the ledge, this whole room must have been facing out over the ravine right below them. Now they again faced eas, out toward the steep mountains, but this time they did so from within the rock.

This common area, as it clearly was, was populated from side to side by groups of Fo-ror and Ja-lal gathered around small tables, with the relaxed energy of any Lodon tower hub.

Luja was clinging to Dayn's arm. "This is amazing," ve exhaled. "Look at everybody."

"How many pyrsi live here?" Dime managed to ask.

"We don't like to be specific, but it's equivalent to many of the larger towns on both sides." Bown beamed at the group's reaction. "We call this place 'Central,' but it's just one room of the larger complex."

Dayn had craned to look around at the stone wall and ceiling. "Old wear. No fissures or flaking. It's all natural, isn't it?"

"As all-natural as I am," Bown chuckled. "Which is to say, yes, mostly. The fairies found it first, and somehow we've managed to keep it a secret. It helps to be almost off the map, but still, we're very protective."

Ve shifted. "I do need to brief you on the rules. The Underground is an open community, and though I'm sort of tasked to run the administration, we mostly self-govern here. You're free to go where you please, outside of occupied living spaces. Basic etiquette is requested and highly valued. And you can send no communications outside. We have room for more pyrsi if you have someone who'd like to join us, but I'd need to explain the protocols more at that point. I'm sure you're tired, walking all that way."

While Dime had been open about her past, she decided not to mention they hadn't walked the whole way. Not really having a true sense of Fo-ror valence, she knew enough to know her level of power was rare. But maybe not enough to know how rare.

She stared out at the expansive gathering space. Other than being carved from natural stone, perhaps by a long-ago water flow that had changed course or almost as if an old canyon could have been rolled to its side, its layout reminded her of the luxury decks atop the norside towers of the city. The space was dotted with tables, some alone and some pushed together, sheltered on top by the stone overhang, and then open to the air on the entire front side. A vast view presented itself from anywhere in the room, sweeping out to the broad slopes of the mountain range.

Sol angled inward with stunning flair, allowing those near the metal safety fence to bask in the full warmth of the daylight, while leaving the far back, where Dime and the others stood, in almost an evening glow.

As one would have to be in the mountains, on the far side of the ravine, to see them—and pyrsi simply didn't go there; it wasn't even considered Sol's Reach—this bustling, beautiful space was left entirely hidden from the mainstreets of the Ja-lal or Fo-ror culture.

Nor did it reflect either. The pyrsi Dime saw, working, sharing a snack, deeply involved in what looked like a game of realms, or relaxed back in their seats engaged in conversation, did not simply look like a group of Ja-lal and Fo-ror had been mixed together into a room. This was much more.

Their cultures swirled, mingled, and expanded here. Like Bown's chin hair, and how ve'd not remarked on her own growing crop, pyrsi here wore a mixture of clothing and accessories. While the Ja-lal seemed mostly to shave their heads as in Sol's Reach, some wore loose headscarves or small caps, something she'd never seen before. And the Fo-ror, while mostly donned in traditional robes, mixed in elements of Ja-lal mechanics, some wearing large timepieces or custom-made eyewear.

It was hard not to stare.

"So this is it," Bown said proudly. "We came here because we wanted freedom. And so we built it ourselves."

If Dime was supposed to feel joy at these words, her reaction was guilt. Guilt for a society that would push pyrsi away to live in hiding, rather than let them bloom as they were.

And she'd thought Sol's Reach was welcoming to differences. Turns out, it was open to *some* differences.

She mused on this as Bown led them down a series of passage-ways, lit brightly with glowstones. They stopped outside of a door, where Bown excused verself a take to check on available rooms. Setting off again, the group continued on, down the corridors and past the occasional junction, opening to ramps leading up or down. The passages in between were lined with framed doorways, some holding wooden doors, and others simply covered with hanging cloth, like the Fo-ror entrance curtains.

Stopping at one with a door, Bown opened it and gestured

them into a generous suite. While windowless, and Dime did love windows, it was one of the most beautifully decorated rooms she'd ever seen, leveraging both the aesthetic and the practicality of each culture. Simple wooden chairs, mats woven of reeds, and a curved stone bar accented the wide space. The stonework was cut to accentuate natural veins of crystal, and polished to a shine.

Bown turned to Dime, discomfort in vis eyes. "This is a Ja-lal setup, with lamps and not furnished for wings. I don't mean to offend. If you'd like us to—"

"No, this is wonderful. Thank you so much."

Bown relaxed. "I'll have a trimming kit sent in, since the grooming stand just has razors." Ve had glanced down at the top of her head.

Dime hadn't considered the idea of trimming hair, and wondered if fairies did so even while keeping it long. "Oh, thank you. You're very kind. The hair is new for me." She ran her fingers through it. "I'll confess I'm not really sure how to trim it. So far, this is just how it's grown."

Bown smiled. "Plenty of pyrsi here would love to help you out. Soon you'll want to brush it, too, at least I think that's the texture you've got."

Brush? Dime rubbed up top. Yeah, it was really growing now.

"It looks great," Bown offered. Ve patted vis own chin. "I'm trying to bring this back. If you'll look around, you see I haven't succeeded. But, eh. It's called a beard. Turns out, it used to be a masc thing for solies." At their confused expressions, he clarified. "For Ja-lal. Here we're called solies. Anyway, I'm going through a masc phase myself, and I've grown attached to it."

"I like it," Luja said from behind. "I wonder if I could grow one."

Dime had a sudden thought that Luja wasn't just talking about biology or hormones, but perhaps Ja-lal valence. Why this made her uncomfortable, she didn't know.

"Now, the kita—" Bown didn't seem to know how to address it. Dime understood. It was unusual for an animal to live in a pyrsi's space, but Agni stayed by her choice, seeming to prefer the company and shelter to outdoor living. Or maybe she'd just bonded to Tum; she never stayed away too long.

"It sounds strange, but she lives with us," Dime explained. "She's used to tower living in Lodon, so we'll make it work."

Bown shrugged. "Alright, then. Well, as the fairies say, I'll get out of your hair. Two rooms are through there: one for you and a smaller one for the ch'pyr." Ve turned to Tum. "If you like gaming, we've got a bunch of gamemakers here." Tum nodded with enthusiasm, and ve laughed. "More than we probably need! So whatever you'd like brought in, we'll find it. Or if you'd like, you can join a club."

Dime was confused by vis count of their group, but ve was talking again.

"And you, Burge Luja, we'll put you right next door, so you aren't far away from this crew. I'm sure you'll want to keep tabs on them." Ve grinned.

Oh. Dime clamped her mouth shut and tried to appear nonchalant as Bown led Luja back out into the hall.

It seemed they were going to be there at least a little while, so Dime made herself start unpacking her things, sorting which would stay in the living area, and which would go back into the bedroom. With a *thunk*, she placed Rock's owl on a shelf to one side. There was no mantle here, so it would have to do.

Bown's head popped back in through the open doorway. "Ve's all set up. Right there if you need ver. Get whatever rest you need. We'll be here. If you need me, just holler."

"Thank you, Bown. We're so grateful for your hospitality," Dayn said. Bown nodded.

"Yes, thank you," Dime added, as the pyr left and shut the door behind ver.

After her last bout of rest on the makeshift mattress in the old woods, their softly-stuffed mattress here felt like sleeping on a cloud in one of her father's mystical story worlds. She rose, found a beautiful common wash area where she could shower and clean off, and moseyed back to their suite.

Agni was stretched out across the floor, her paws curling back and forth; it amazed Dime how much larger or smaller she could appear by changing her position. Tum was just waking up, so she made sure she knew about the larger washroom and offered her any help she needed. Dayn must already have found it, as he was setting his razor down on the grooming stand as she walked in, rubbing a thin layer of oil across his scalp.

"Sorry. No hair or beard for me."

Dime snorted. "Don't be sorry. Be you!"

"Right now, *me*, is thinking we need to find where food is served. Because if the Underground is foodless, I probably will be Abovegrounding again shortly."

"I'm with you. Tum's in the washroom. Have you checked on Luja?"

"I'm here, Ma-ma."

Dime turned. She hadn't even noticed Luja lounging back with a book, vis feet propped up on a stool. Dime wasn't sure that stool was meant for feet.

"Do all the fairies use those stone lights, like the ones in the hall? Instead of lamps?" Ve pointed to the small lamp to vis side.

Dime nodded. "Yes. I mean, who knows if they *all* do, but yes, they are what they use instead of lamps."

"It kind of makes me mad," ve said.

"How's that?" Dime asked, as Dayn turned to listen.

"Well, they're better than lamps. They don't take fuel to burn, the light is steadier, and they're safer, as far as I can tell. If we just worked together, everyone could have them."

Dime was considering how to respond when there was a rapping at their door. "Come in," she said, expecting to see the blue beard of

Bown, though if ve really was running the place, ve'd probably be too busy to keep stopping by.

Instead, she was shocked as Volana's swaying figure swung through the door, curved with pregnancy, her ribboned gown looking no less lovely in the warm glow of the inside space than it had in the green-hued light of the forest. While the furnishings hadn't been set up for wings, the room was large enough, and Volana's multi-hued wings swished behind her as she entered.

"Volana!" Dime was shocked to see the fairy, and felt at a loss for words. "You're here!"

"So nice to see you again," Dayn said, moving forward to offer her a stool. Not the one Luja was using.

"I am. Before you ask, I had no idea about this place. It's astonishing, is it not?"

"We only saw the first room. And my parents are still getting ready to go back out," Luja interjected.

"Oh, well you are in for a surprise. Maybe we can go together?"

"Do you know where the food is?"

"It seems we share priorities," Volana answered. "Also, I've been thirsty more often." She patted her midsection.

Eating was a priority they all shared, Dime never having turned down a meal herself. "How does food work here, anyway?" Dime asked. "Is there a grocer? Do they take paynotes?" Dime still had a few of the paynotes Ella had given her.

"No, no," Volana shook her head.

Dime remembered that all Fo-ror had been raised to consider paynotes unethical, so she hoped Volana wasn't bothered by the casual mention. She thought she was more open-minded than that. Dime still wasn't convinced there was anything wrong with paynotes, besides. But she was willing to listen.

"I am not sure of what a grocer is, but all the food is managed by the kitchens. They will prepare it for you, or there are a few smaller kitchens where you can prepare your own. But only if you want to—the kitchens are open all the time. There are no rations; if there is a shortage of something, pyrsi are told and adjust.

"Who works in the kitchen?" Luja asked, leaning forward with interest. "Who gets the food? And how?"

"Pyrsi here contribute what they are good at and what they like to do. If something isn't being done, then they ask for more pyrsi to cover it. For things not enough pyrsi want to do, they split the tasks and take volunteers."

"And that works?" Dime would have to think through this.

"It seems to. Remember, I've not been here long."

That was true; it had only been a turn since she'd been in the forest with Volana, at the gathering with the top two Seats. Well, three, as it'd turned out.

"When I talked to your friend, Ella, she told me of this place. Sort of. Explained that it was a secret, but said that she trusted me. She told me her own story, briefly, as time was short. Of her spouse, since she had mentioned her at the gathering." Volana paused a stride, her eyes downcast. "She said if I am working within the Foundry, this place would give me more perspective to consider. She trusted me, and so I trusted her. I am supposed to be at shift already. I did leave them a note saying I would be unavailable." She winced.

Dime was embarrassed for not having thought that through. Of course Volana couldn't stay here for any reasonable period and still make all of her work shifts. And in a system without paynotes, one was simply expected to be where assigned. Dime had left her own career. That was her fault. Or whatever one would call it. In Volana's case, the fairy was truly putting herself at risk for the cause of peace. She hoped that wasn't a justification for arrest, but that wasn't something she wanted to ask. Dime took in a breath.

"Is Uchitar here, then?"

Volana grimaced. "He is working some issues out with . . . pyrsi close to him. I did not like leaving him." She didn't seem to want to say more, and so Dime didn't press.

"But," Volana continued, her voice raising in energy again, "your friends are here. Ador, and Hin. And now you. We can all attend a gathering together. There is a party scheduled, later."

"A party?" Tum had rushed into the room, her face glowing at the sight of the fairy. "Hi, Volana!" Tum leaned back against a wall and reached out her arms.

Volana swooped down to give Tum a hug, murmuring something to her.

Wait, Ador and Hin were here? Dime was still patching all these pieces together.

Rising from her crouch, Volana returned to the stool.

"Ador and Hin are here too?" Dayn asked, though aloud in his case. "But not Batu?"

"No, Batu is in Lodon."

Dime noted the tilted way that Volana pronounced her city, as if the vowels weren't quite right. She wondered if she was saying Pito oddly. She'd remember to ask.

Volana looked wistful. Dime had heard she'd been in a relationship. She hoped it was going well. Seeming to intuit the unspoken thought, Volana smiled. "I am seeing someone, and like Batu, he is back in Pito. His name is Ma'Eytanii. He's . . . wonderful." Now she could not hide her joy. "Even my mothers like him." She rolled her eyes.

"It is too bad; he would like it here. Everyone is so friendly in this place, and they make it so easy to meet pyrsi and socialize. There is what they call 'Central,' that you saw, and it is always open for general meeting. Then there are many gathering areas and lounges, with and without ferm or food, and some where ch'pyrsi are not allowed. There are social spans for friendships, families, asexuals, demisexuals, extrasexuals, aromantics, polyromantics, specific attractions, and all sorts of combinations of each." She flung back a hand. "I'm sure I'm missing so many, but you get the point.

"There are discussion groups for things like physical and mental conditions, life phases, and such. Then there are interest rooms, for debate, study, writing, gaming—" She'd waved her hand with each new listing, and now she held it still. "Again, it would take me turns just to learn all that goes on and cycles to describe it.

"I went to an asexual gathering, which was not only for dating, but any conversation, and everyone was so nice and welcoming. Eytanii—he is also asexual—would have loved it. It seems everything here is dedicated to making sure pyrsi can thrive being exactly who they are. Here, they work through life together. Whether it is sharing happiness or dealing with difficulty." She stopped, out of breath. Luja poured her a glass of water from a pitcher stand, which she accepted with a grateful nod.

"Just think if that was everyone's goal," Dayn mused, having helped Tum next to him on a padded bench. "Did you hear all that?" he asked her, before sharing a grin with Luja.

In that moment, Dime couldn't help but feel a twinge of isolation. There would be no gathering, she figured, for pyrsi like her. No place to talk about what it was like to be—what had Bown called it—a soly, while living in the modified body of a fairy. Still, Volana and Dayn sounded excited, so she kept this to herself.

"The complex is enormous, almost a city," Volana continued. "Most of the common spaces open on the side of the rock face. There is an entrance in the ravine, accessible for the Ja-lal, and then pathways run down to Heartland sand on the other side of the cliff. Lower that way, there is an accessible outdoor area, where pyrsi may practice climbing or flying skills, or may play at physical sport. And there is an observation deck." She waved an arm. "If you can fly, you are not supposed to fly in front of the complex itself."

Dime could understand that. She wouldn't feel as comfortable in the common spaces, not knowing which fairies were flying past, looking in. She had a sudden moment of considering what it would be like for fairies to live in Lodon. Maybe that's why fairies had curtains.

Volana finished her water, then turned to the room. "Would you like to go see it?"

Meeting Dayn's eyes, Dime relaxed at his warm gaze. He'd probably sensed her apprehension. She smiled, so grateful they were here together.

"I think that sounds fantastic," Dayn said, helping Tum into her chair. By habit, really, as Tum could get in on her own. She never seemed to mind a helping hand from her Da-da. Dime basked in that feeling of warmth as they all filed out into the hallway. She noticed Luja gazing at the glowstones.

As Bown had said, Central was just a small piece of this city built into the stone. It was a city, she realized, not of the scope of Lodon or Pito by far, but certainly expansive and populated enough to stand by the title. And with a culture of its own.

As they walked, and highlighted by Tum's loud exclamations of each new discovery, she noticed that while Volana had mentioned ch'pyrsi, there weren't nearly as many around as Dime would have expected in a residential area. She resolved to ask about that, if she thought she could without offending. Mostly to make sure there weren't any issues with Tum staying here.

Everyone stopped and said hello as she passed, offering greetings as well as fanning their fingers, or the curved finger gesture that seemed to be the equivalent in the Heartland. Some, maybe used to doing both for so long, merged the two, fanning somewhat and curving somewhat.

Much to Dayn's satisfaction—and Dime's as well, though she didn't express it over Dayn and Volana's banter—there was a huge common space dedicated to eating, also with a wide outside view. It was night now, and a string of tiny glowstones lined the safety fence, swinging gently as pyrsi passed by. Outside, the skystones reflected soft light over the silhouette of the mountains beyond. It still awed Dime, to think she was looking out at a land where no one lived. Though, who knew. She hadn't thought anyone lived here.

The kitchen menu was written on a large board, with items added or removed as the menu shifted. After an excited discussion, they selected to share a huge bowl of twirling noodles, topped with fresh curlshrooms and thin strands of a mélange of different roots, with a savory seed crunch topping. Each pyr was served their own cup of a rich, salted broth, which they could drink separately or use to soak their noodles.

They offered to help clean the dishes, but, hearing they were new, the servers insisted otherwise, saying there was plenty of time for them to find a role. Eager to see more and, Dime thought, hopefully find Ador, they set out to explore the vast complex.

After a while, when Luja and Tum had broken off together, Volana led Dime and Dayn to what appeared to be a tavern, filled with pyrsi. Volana ushered them in, saying they had the best freshly squeezed juices, and Dime, who offered to bring back something for Dayn as well, walked up to a countertop to place an order.

For a flash, she wasn't sure whether the bartender was Ja-lal or Fo-ror. She wasn't sure why, because at a second glance, xe was dressed much as a traditional Ja-lal, with criss-crossing tattoos, and a cheery apron tied over xyr tunic.

"Hello," she said. "I'm Fe'Dime. It's my first time here. Are there any—restrictions on what to order?" It sounded funny, but being used to paynotes and prices, she didn't want to misstep.

"Ma'Klein," he greeted. "Nice to meet you. No restrictions you aren't used to."

That was a strange answer, but she sensed no sarcasm in his tone. Maybe some humor.

At her pause, he seemed to catch himself. "I keep my bars well-stocked, so whatever you'd like I can try to make." He nodded cheerfully and tapped the counter.

"What do you recommend? Any specials?" She bit her lip, realizing she wasn't sure what a special would be in a place with no prices. She hoped that wasn't offensive. Here, she'd been telling everyone that they were all the same, but that didn't seem to follow. Maybe it was more that they were equal. Not necessarily the same.

Klein grinned. "If you mean my specialty, yes, I do know how to make the perfect Aviation. It's a ferm."

"Alright, two of those, then." She wasn't sure if he'd said *avian* as it had sounded mushed at the end, but a drink named after flight seemed oddly apropos.

Soon, he returned, shaking together a pair of large metal cups. Parting them, an indigo-hued liquid poured down into two stemmed glasses. Or maybe it was violet. Either way, it reminded her of wings.

"Thank you, these look wonderful." She hesitated, not wanting to be rude about not tipping. She figured she might as well ask. "Is anything customary to offer?"

He paused as if remembering something, then turned back. "New from Lodon, then? No, nothing at all. Just enjoy it while it's cold is all."

"That, I can do," she said, giving the pyr a last nod before walking cautiously back to the table. To her surprise, they'd moved to a larger one, where not just Volana and Dayn sat, but others as well. By their looks, there were three Fo-ror and one Ja-lal, though the differences were more blurred here. Wings were a fairly certain tell, though as Dime certainly could attest, one never knew for sure.

"Ok, I can get this," Volana started. "Ma'Fotori and his spouse, Ma'Tesajin. Fe'Perg. And Fe'Kimbaia." Always a diplomat, Volana's skill with names did not surprise her.

While they all exchanged greetings, Dime handed Dayn his drink and took a sip of her own, pausing first to admire the floating sheets of ice across the iridescent surface. As the others spoke, she looked back up.

"So we both moved here with our Ja-lal soulmates." Fotori and Tesajin each laughed, and Fotori continued. "Then we met each other. By the time that all played out, we were happy here. And we'd made friends. Happy enough we saw no reason to return to the forest."

"I do miss it," Tesajin said.

The comment caught Fotori off guard, and he placed a hand on his spouse's arm.

Next to them, Kimbaia sighed. "It's like this sometimes when new pyrsi arrive. I mean, look around. It's perfect here. Everyone who's here wanted to be here, and we all have a disposition that appreciates individuality and community, and so things run pretty smoothly. But, Ada-ji is beautiful outside. We gained so much, but we gave up much too." Kimbaia tipped back her drink.

Though Kimbaia had wings and hair, Dime noticed that she also held a few facial tattoos, bordering the edge of her lightly-tinted braids and curved around the hair of one brow. No, she couldn't quite imagine her walking around Pito with those. Maybe someturn. One of the markings looked familiar, but Dime wasn't going to stare. She took another sip of the avian, admiring the subtlety of its flavors.

"I miss ch'pyrsi," Perg added. "I mean, I'm not interested in parenting, myself, but I miss having them around." Dime had the impression she was leaving something unsaid. Family members, maybe, on the outside. Dime thought of her own children, wandering around somewhere.

"I did wonder about that," Dime said, hoping since Perg had broached the topic, her statement wasn't rude. Volana might be interested too. "In Lodon, there are more ch'pyrsi."

"We don't get many parents here," Fotori explained. "From a practical standpoint, families with children are less likely to be out where they might meet someone from the other side. And those who do, on chance, are usually warned before visiting about the isolation factor. It's a big secret to keep, being here."

"I don't think we're meant to keep secrets this big," his spouse interjected. "If you think about it, it's the antithesis of the place. Come here where there's no big secrets except the existence of the whole place?"

"So," Fotori continued, "over time, a pyr's child could leave. Pyrsi reaching their point of decision are always given that choice. And when they do leave, they always intend to slip away from time to time and visit in secret. But it gets harder. They don't. They find a life on the outside, one that won't allow secret absences or extra time off. That's a big choice for a child to make about family, so prior to inviting a parent, we warn xem."

"They usually stay where they are," Perg explained. "It's just too big of a cliff for a parent to jump over."

Dime squinted.

"Well, our friends are here," Perg said, tapping Kimbaia's arm. She looked back to Dime, Dayn, and Volana. "Just a group of feminine pyrsi that like to get together. We call it drink club."

Dime turned to the side to see a mix of Fo-ror and Ja-lal pushing tables together and bringing over drinks. Dayn started to speak, Dime figured to compliment the delightfully literal name, but the fe'pyrsi had already started walking away.

"Well, we should be going as well," Fortori said, offering his spouse an arm to rise. Tesajin reached for a cane and then stood, his wings stretching out slowly behind him. "It was lovely to meet you. I'm sure we'll see you around."

"Yes, likewise," Dayn said. Once they were alone again, he turned back to Dime.

"I know you've dealt with this more, but is it still odd to you that the fairies aren't just not mythical, they are entirely . . . normal?" He stopped, seeming to wonder if Dime or Volana would be bothered by his comment. "Volana, I don't mean anything by it." And then to Dime, "I'm sorry, I just think of you as you."

"I know. I prefer it." Dime said. And she did. At least, with someone like Dayn, who she knew would adjust to and want to understand her developing identity.

"I hope I didn't offend," he said to Volana, who had indeed been quiet, though certainly before Dayn's comment.

"No, not even a little. I'm like you, really." She adjusted on her seat with some discomfort. "One day I am open-minded to meeting Ja-lal. Now I am surrounded by them." She nodded at Dayn. "Like you, I am happy with this. But it is . . . a change."

"I know," he said. "Especially our hairless scalps?" He rubbed his head.

Dime may have been the only one to catch Volana's slight wince, as she immediately offered a broad, warm smile. "It is beautiful, now that I see it."

"So," Dime interrupted, her thoughts still churning. "Am I not doing this right? Should I have told them right there about our goals?"

"No," Volana and Dayn said in unison.

"Not here," Dayn added.

"No, I don't think so," Volana continued. "Just as we are adjusting, they will need to adjust. We have time, I think."

Dime wasn't sure they did have time. She'd been grasped by Neimano's guard. She'd seen the pushing at the gates, and the attack on the plains. She'd been attacked by Neimano's valence—twice—and seen what Stern Eyes had done to save them. She knew the newts were considering marching to the Heartland, considering using the Violence if the Fo-ror tried to stop them. The one they called Leader could be organizing it now.

"I don't know," was all she murmured, overwhelmed. She resolved, soon, to begin spreading their message. Her greatest fear, now, even with just a little sense of the culture, was how to get pyrsi to come out into the open who had spent their whole lives feeling constrained to stay here, together. And how they might deal with facing the imperfections of the larger world again. Yet, the larger world would benefit from these pyrsi.

She was lost in these thoughts, as Volana and Dayn had a lengthy conversation regarding the construction and use of the Pito canals. Finishing her drink and setting it in the wash tray, she followed as they walked down the halls, now talking about rain patterns or something. "Oh, let's stop here," Volana said with excitement, looking through a pulled-back curtain. "There are some of my friends from the last gathering." She pointed across the room.

"I mean, we have asexual gatherings in the Heartland too, but it is more complicated, due to the restrictions of class. Here, I've learned, no one cares about that. If you're here, maybe you can be friends. Maybe you can be more. I just like . . . talking to pyrsi who understand."

Dime's father, Gorg, was aromantic. That wasn't the same, yet Dime couldn't imagine him enjoying an aromantic bar party to save his life. A corner-ball hall, all turn. Pyrsi were different, of course.

She felt like a speck of dust in the light of Volana's glow as the fairy whisked Dayn and her around to introduce them to her new friends. Finally, they sat along a curved seat, and Volana brought over glasses of water and a plate of small fruits and mixed berries.

She sat down with a sigh.

"Are you ok?" Dime whispered.

"I am perfect."

Dime didn't pry, and Volana sighed again.

"Eytanii is not here." Volana plucked a berry from the plate. "I wish he could be here to enjoy this. I worry, since I am skipping my shifts, if he will be upset."

On top of Volana's schedule as a cleaner, Dime knew she gave tireless devotion to helping those addicted to tzetz. She also knew Volana was harassed for it; Dime had witnessed this the first time they'd met. Like in Lodon, tzetz use was a crime in Pito, and so mocking association with it was considered noble by some, rather than the Violence, which it obviously was.

Volana worked a lot of shifts, and spent enough time working at the canals, and now she was risking her status and freedom for a cause that didn't even involve her directly. Any pyr who didn't admire that wouldn't be a good match, but of course Dime wouldn't say so. She didn't even know the situation. "If he understands you . . . it will be alright." She hoped that was ok.

"I hope so. Eytanii will be such a good father." Her eyes cut over, realizing what she had said. "There is nothing settled. I— I—"

Dime could hear the panic in her voice. "No, no," Dime comforted the younger fe'pyr. "We won't say anything. And I'm certain that he will be." To herself, she noted she was going to have to meet this ma'pyr. Not that Volana, of all pyrsi, needed any protection, she thought with a grin, admiring the fairy's raised chin and set eyes.

Dayn reached over and squeezed her hand, out of view, and Dime squeezed it back.

The fe'pyrsi who Volana had previously met joined them, and Volana seemed to settle back into her usual confidence. Watching the Ja-lal and Fo-ror gathered at each table, Dime realized one big difference here from what she had seen in the Heartland: no one was using valence. That was something Volana had not mentioned, either.

Yet, she knew the subject was openly discussed in Fo-ror culture, and except for herself and Dayn, the fe'pyrsi at their table were Fo-ror. So she asked them.

"If it's not impolite, it doesn't seem that pyrsi use much valence here. Is that an agreed rule, or just part of the culture?" Perhaps rules regarding valence were discussed as part of the entry briefing; Bown may not have thought they applied to her.

The fe'pyrsi seemed to stare a moment, and so she added, "I was born in the Heartland myself, and have fairy valence, but I've lived my life entirely in Sol's Reach. I've visited the Heartland just these last turns, and seen how casually valence was used in the Seats' complex, and then more selectively other places."

Volana's eyes widened, reflecting her surprise that Dime revealed this truth in front of the others. Or, truths, she supposed.

"How interesting," the first fe'pyr said, lifting a glass. "And no, there's no strict rule against valence here, as some pyrsi need it for certain tasks. We keep the stones lit, and it aids some pyrsi with specific needs. But the use of valence can be detected. Even small uses over this many pyrsi might draw attention. We don't want attention. So pyrsi are sensitive." She brought the drink to her lips. Her friend nodded.

Just then, a familiar face poked in through the room's curtain. Seeing him and practically ignoring whether Dayn followed her, Dime issued a quick thanks and hurried off toward the corridor.

"Ador!" she said, as she stepped outside. "Volana said you were here! Did Ella send you also?"

"Ella? Ah, so she's who told you. Bown asked when I arrived if I'd been the one to direct you here, which was a shock considering I was going to ask him if I could invite you! No, I've been here a few times over the cycles. One of the few who's allowed in and out without suspicion—a privilege I've done my best to honor. I couldn't talk about it at your den, but I wanted to. And Volana, here too. It was a nice surprise to see her." Ador pulled the curtain to glance into the lounge. "Speaking of whom, looks like she and Dayn are making their departure with your acquaintances a bit less abrupt."

Dime winced. She supposed she had just popped up from the table. But with everything she'd been through, she found immeasurable comfort with her friends.

"Hin is here also," he said. "It's his first time, and he's agitated. I figured there was no better way to shake his disquiet with the fairies than dropping him in the middle of some of the nicest, most open-minded ones in Ada-ji."

Nodding, Dime could imagine this would be a shock to the younger ma'pyr. "Is he handling it alright?"

"Ehh—" Ador shrugged. "He'll get there. I can't imagine anyone not falling in love with the freedom here. If I can just get him to stop hiding in our suite."

"It's sort of a strange place, I suppose. Volana seems a little thrown off, and I didn't think anything would do that."

"A lot of fairies get uncomfortable at first, being in a place where it's not easy to fly," he noted.

"I feel that way about being so inside," Dime said, understanding. "Even in a tower, you can step outside sometimes. Feel Sol."

Ador looked through the curtain again, checking that Dayn and Volana were still near the table. "She's also missing the pyr she's been dating. It brings me back, sometimes. I love my life, but the look of someone who's met someone new has grown so foreign to me. It reminds me of my age in ways that other things do not."

She knew that their old friend was monogamous with his spouse, Batu, and they'd been married quite a while. "I suppose it's one of those things about committing," she said. "Besides, I couldn't imagine you dating."

Ador didn't answer right away, as Dayn and Volana joined them. After a tight hug to his best friend, Ador reached out his fingertips to meet Volana's, and each bowed.

"I need the washroom more than I should admit," Volana said with a laugh. "I will see you soon."

"Yes," Dayn said. "We'll see you. Stop by anytime."

As Volana left, Ador grinned at Dayn. "Your spouse was just saying she couldn't imagine me dating. As if Batu and I met in the playcourt."

Dayn shook his head, and Dime grew annoyed, though only superficially. *Ma'pyr secrets.*

"Well, I'll let her figure that out," Dayn said. "It's so good to see you here! I fear, though, you've been following me."

Ador laughed.

"You know where we're staying?"

"I do," Ador said.

"Stop by later." Dayn turned to Dime. "Don't begrudge me my coddling, but I'd like to go find our children." He stepped forward to give Dime a little peck on the cheek. Which she appreciated a lot, her eyes following her wonderful spouse as he walked back down the hallway.

"Want to see our quarters?" Dime said. "Maybe they'll be there soon. I know the kids will be so excited to see you."

"And I, them." Ador smiled. "Sure." He paused. "You don't remember how to get back, do you?"

"I don't." Dime laughed, and Ador headed off, leading the way. And soon they arrived at what Dime was glad to see was their room. This time she thought she had it.

They sat down at the table, across from each other.

"Windows," she said, still considering her thoughts about not being able to go outside.

"I agree," Ador responded. "This place is wildly idyllic, but there is something too symbolic about not being able to see Ada-ji from within."

Of course Ador made everything poetic.

"Ella did send me," she confirmed, reaching back to their earlier conversation. "And Volana. She's a meddler. Anyway, I think she's right. No, I *know* she's right," Dime corrected. "I need to learn how to talk to pyrsi. Though, I suppose that's your specialty, so I'm glad you're here." Dime scrunched her nose. "You know, she probably figured that too, harm it. Well, anyway." She threw her hands up in the air. "How do I talk to pyrsi?"

Ador grinned. "You start talking." Seeing Dime's glare, he continued. "Sometimes pyrsi don't speak because they don't know how to speak perfectly." He leaned in. "Something I've learned the hard way over all these cycles of working this. We have to keep speaking. The pyrsi who are eager to shut you down because you don't say things the way they want—let them return to their cults. Don't fuel them. Speak anyway. Listen. Listen to pyrsi who engage. Speak to those who will listen." He drifted off, as if remembering something.

Dime wasn't sure what pyrsi he meant, or what cults. Perhaps such as Sol's Pillars; she'd seen a group mentality at work there.

"Anyway," he continued, "we'll get some events scheduled at Central. Bown will be happy to help; just talk to ver."

"More has happened. We should talk."

Ador straightened in his seat.

"First, I think Ja-lal have valence too."

As her friend liked to maintain a certain decorum, she was not used to seeing him freeze, fully stunned, the way he did at her news. Maybe he didn't . . . no, he did believe her. That explained the expression.

"It's internal," she continued. "You can't make the table move, but perhaps you could make yourself strong enough to move the table. I don't know, yet. It's a lot to figure out. Luja and Tum have been working it."

They both opened their mouths at the same time, and now Ador shifted forward like a ch'pyr. "There's *more*?"

"The newts too. They have valence. This is a huge secret."

Ador held quiet, seeming to note there was something of even further concern in her expression.

"The pyr who cut off my wings is one of the Fo-ror leaders. Well, you know what they're called. The current Third Seat. He found us in the forest, and two of my newt friends were there." She could see him mouth out *newt friends*, but he did not interrupt. "He used . . . the Violence against us." Taking a breath, she made herself say it. "He attacked us. And, to save us, one of the newts attacked him back. I'm not even sure if she meant to; it may have been like . . . what happened to me outside the city. When they grabbed Luja." Dime felt the knot in her stomach returning. "We're hoping he thinks I'm the one who attacked him.

"But she did it, the newt I mean—without question. And I'm worried whether or not that will push the newts over the edge. They've been debating its use, anyway. Pyrsi aren't supposed to know any of this. But the fairies are actively harming them, even without direct contact. With their net." She noted Ador's mix of expressions. "They have a fence that keeps the newts out of most of the forest. The newts are living on the sandy shores of the Heartland, but it's not healthy for them there. So," she concluded. "What are your thoughts?"

Ador was quiet for a stride as he settled against the chair back. "Tum had mentioned something, but she was going on as you know, and I didn't grasp the full extent of it. And that must have been before this . . . incident."

"It was," Dime agreed. "But Tum was there. And Luja."

He paused. "It wouldn't be right to push the newts into the Violence because of our actions against them."

Dime considered his words, and realized he meant the broader set of pyrsi as *we*, not just the Fo-ror. For some reason, that heartened her.

"I don't know if I have the answers either," he continued. "I think we should focus on getting your coalition together. I agree with you. It's time."

"Maybe it should have been time before," Dime muttered.

Ador paused, and Dime worried by his tight expression she'd offended him. He shook it off, forcing a smile. "But we'll do it now. I . . . would leave the newts out at first. Get the coalition talking, then make the net issue a first topic between us."

"It's not just the Fo-ror," Dime was quick to note. "Our Circles are conducting boring operations in the sur. Or at least they were. It puts the Heartland at grave risk."

Ador rubbed his temples. "All these cycles, and it's like I haven't done a thing."

"No." It hurt Dime to hear someone who had spent his life trying to be on the right side of things harm himself mentally for not having done enough. Her heart ached now, along with the knot in her stomach. "Maybe because of all your work, pyrsi will listen now. Maybe the turning of the shadows will be a result of your light."

Ador started to laugh.

"What?" Dime huffed.

"You're always accusing me of being poetic."

"Well. Maybe I learned it from you. Anyway, we need to get to Bown?"

"We do. Ve's with us, Dime. Ve just has a very delicate balance to maintain here."

"I don't know. Everyone seems happy." But, that wasn't true either. She remembered the overt sadness pyrsi she'd barely met had displayed when talking about the outside world.

"It's tiring." Ador's shoulders visibly drooped, even padded in the traditional Ja-lal style. "Pyrsi either want an easy solution or they don't want to think about it. Pyrsi like us who know the solution isn't easy but work for it anyway—we get attacked from all sides."

Attacked. Dime winced at the harsh language, but, you know, why wasn't their continued prejudice and separation the Violence too? Why wasn't the Free Winds being seen as a threat by the Circles a form of the Violence? Ella had said something similar.

"I'll always be here with you," she offered. It was all she could think to say.

"I'm so glad you left that place. I couldn't—" Sighing, he reached his hands over the table and Dime put hers over them. The simple touch was more comfort than she could describe. Then, looking up, she suddenly remembered where she'd seen that tattoo.

"Ador."

"Yes?" Oh, she'd missed the sarcastic tilt of his face.

"Do you know Kimbaia? A fairy here?"

Ador snorted. "We dated a very long time ago, briefly, on my first visit. I had transitioned, and she was struggling with her own identity at the time, though I always saw her for who she was. I was so happy for her when I learned she'd announced."

"You mean announced as fe'pyr? I saw that she had a few tattoos, but one reminded me of yours." Dime usually forgot about this, but Ador had a tattoo that signaled he hadn't always been identified as ma'pyr.

"Yeah. I told her she didn't need to do it, I mean, I marked myself out of pure pride." He touched his own tattoo. "She said the tribute was a form of thanks. She's adventurous, that one." The gleam in his eyes was pyrsonal, and Dime glanced away.

"Stop it!" Ador said. "It's like Dayn said—I was allowed to date before my marriage. Didn't you? I mean, I can understand Dayn being a first love—he has his charm—but I wouldn't have guessed it."

Dime winced. "No, not the first. But I didn't date a lot. Always found myself too different from other pyrsi. Too serious. I couldn't explain it then, and I don't know if I could now." She still didn't look up.

"Oh, I could. Anyway, I dated many interesting pyrsi."

There was something he wasn't telling her. She raised her head. "Ok, I'm not asking, but there's clearly someone else that I know. Who did you date?"

He leaned forward. "Sala."

"What?" Not only had her best friend founded the most influential and, now she realized, necessary organization in Sol's Reach, but he had *dated the Light?*

Ador looked delighted as festival at her reaction. Just for that, she tried to tamp it down. "Oh, of course you did. I mean, I talked to her the other day. Seems lovely."

"Did you?" He took the comment as serious, which it was. "She divorced a while back," he added, a small sadness clouding his eyes. "It must be terribly isolating, in her role."

"Ferala mentioned having a spouse. High Seat Ferala. He seemed happy, from what I could tell."

"Pyrsi are different. Anyway, Sala is a lovely fe'pyr. A good leader, or at least has the skills to be. She just can't unscrew her head around to see that maintaining peace isn't the same thing as maintaining comfort. Anyway. It's been a long time since we've spoken. A very long time." Now Ador didn't meet her gaze.

Dime considered how actively the Circles tried to keep the influence of the Free Winds to a minimum. She considered how much that must hurt Ador, at least lingering somewhere in the background. Then, she considered how they'd met. Had Sala been engaged with the Free Winds? Had Sala been here? She wasn't going to ask him that.

Instead, she took out the dice from her pocket, one a rich amethyst and one onyx. The darker one seemed to change as it turned, pure black from some angles, and almost reflecting a bit of the other die's purple from others. They were mesmerizing. "I know I've already thanked you, but can I say again how lovely these are?"

"They were symbolic."

"Well, I'm aware of that," Dime said with a laugh. "But guess what, you can play games with them too."

Accepting her offer, they moved to the comfy chairs in the far corner of the room. Dime pulled over an old wood table, carved with interesting patterns. There, Ador joined her in a variety of dice games, deep into inventing a realms-style back and forth story path when the others finally returned to the suite, Agni trailing behind them. Dime stood and slid the dice back into their pouch, as any hopes of further conversation were definitely out, with her children's excitement to see their honorary auncle.

Volana was not with them, but Luja had come in. Dime hadn't mentioned that ve seemed so grown that Bown had provided ver vis own room, but she figured Luja would work it in somewhere. Maybe better for Ador to hear that from Luja verself.

As Tum excitedly listed everything she'd seen in the Underground thus far, Luja stepped over and leaned in.

"Yes?" Dime rested her head against her child's shoulder, recognizing again that ve was now substantially taller than she was.

"Can we talk to Ador about . . . anything?" Luja murmured the question.

Dime knew that could mean a great many things. At a pause in Tum's story, Dime decided to address it with the room. "I just want to let everyone know—I think we'd all agree that discretion would be wise elsewhere, but there are no secrets from Ador."

Which meant it took Tum about a stride to launch into all the latest on the newts and all her concerns about them as Agni went and curled in a corner. Luja hovered awkwardly next to Dime.

Dime smiled at ver. "You'll have time to talk."

"I wonder if he knows about valence," ve responded. "We aren't practicing ours here, because of the etiquette."

She knew ve meant Ja-lal valence. "I told him. I didn't have the impression he knew." Dime could see from vis eyes it was something ve planned to discuss with him, but she'd already said all topics were on the table. Then, so be it.

Realizing Ador was not going to be free for a while, and with his leave, Dime went on her own to find Bown and get vis advice on setting up some sort of discussion sessions. Bown was reluctant at first. Finally, ve turned to her.

"A few pyrsi come here because they've heard of the lifestyle, or had it glamorized to them by some peddler at the Crossing who made it a point not to live here xemself. And a few come as idealists, eager to experience this radical new model. A new Ada-ji. But most of us come here hurt. We hide that hurt away. We don't talk about it." Ve curled vis lip.

"And we love it here. It really is as great as it must seem. But our hurt has been pushed so far down, that when someone suggests we can just let this go, return to the outside and trust that those same pyrsi won't cause that same hurt—" Ve ran a hand down his beard. "I'm not explaining this well."

"No, you are," Dime said, trying to think through these new angles. "And I think I understand. I'd like to. I'm here to listen as well as to talk. No one should take away your feelings. And maybe here . . . it feels like the hurt is isolated. But it's not. There is pain outside too. Pyrsi can't ignore it anymore, and the peace that the Circles and the Seats tried to maintain is cracking. They see it. They know it."

She paused, wanting to ask ver whether ve'd stay here and continue to live in peace, if ve knew the world outside had returned to war. If ve knew perhaps the pyrsi here could have stopped it. But this was too much burden to place on the few who had resisted normalizing division all along. Dime could only tell them what she'd seen. "You'll let me talk? I'll be clear up front why I'm here."

Bown closed vis eyes.

The reaction to Dime's talks were as mixed as Bown's had been. Some pyrsi listened intently, and others sat with folded arms. Some asked sincere questions, and other questions seemed designed to invoke a particular answer. Some stated oversimplifications as fact, which either set Dime up to look argumentative or concede to a point that she couldn't. Dime did her best to muddle through.

A couple pyrsi had even gotten up and left, though she tried to tell herself maybe they needed the washroom. She was upfront with her goals; though she felt exposed and nervous, she pushed through with recounting what she had seen and her desire to discuss what could be done to help. By the third session, she had a better idea what to expect and how to guard herself against the uncertainties of their reactions. This time, she was hoping enough of the groundwork had been laid that they could actually get to a productive discussion.

She stood almost flush against the safety fence, given how crowded the room was, with word spreading of her story. They hadn't removed the tables, but they were pushed tightly together toward the ravine side of the room, with pyrsi standing behind them.

With a grimace, she'd accepted the step stool they'd offered to raise her up over the others. She held up a hand, and remarked at how well the large space quieted. As she'd already learned, there were natural acoustics to the wide stone room, making it easy to be heard when facing the back, as she was. She wished she could see how she looked, elevated with the nighttime shapes of the mountains behind her. A sudden image of that silhouette framed with wings came into view, and she blinked it away.

"I'll skip a lot of the intro this time, as I know rumors about me have been all over the Underground, even more than they've flown through Lodon."

The crowd responded with a polite laugh. But Dime hadn't meant to joke, often forgetting that the fairies didn't use the word as metaphorically as the solies did. This tripped her a little, but she tried to steady her voice.

"I'm Fe'Dime, and though I'd traveled Sol's Reach some, I spent my life in Lodon, working for the Circles." There was a murmur at this. "I just learned recently that I was born in the Heartland, with the biology of a fairy." She would have said Fo-ror but Bown had warned her pyrsi here took the terms as political, and she'd go further with the common terms of fairy and soly. "And so my valence takes the form of a fairy, even though I am a soly."

Prompted by the wide eyes around her, she realized her stark assertion of being a soly seemed to startle some of the listeners. Oh well, she was.

"I have witnessed widespread feelings of unrest across Ada-ji and pyrsi worrying what change might bring. I've seen incidents broaching the Violence." No matter how many times she said it, this always got a rumble. "My friend, Volana, is here from the Foundry, and my friend, Ador is representing the Free Winds. They can attest to their concerns regarding the Heartland and Sol's Reach, respectively.

"I have met with the leaders of both lands." She paused, letting that reaction settle. "I believe both leaders care deeply about pyrsi, in their own ways, though they feel restricted, or shielded from action. We must work to help them."

"How can you say that?" a voice interrupted.

She looked across at the pyr, a Ja-lal.

"You're as bad as they are. You worked for the Circles, then you come here, uninvited as far as anyone here can tell, and tell us the Light's Circle gives a harm for our well-being? After what they've done and continue to do? Even after your own admission, they are watching the Violence return to our families and doing nothing? You are the Violence. You can get the kill out of here." Several pyrsi around xem let little cheers, and the pyr who'd spoken stared right at her, smiling.

Dime's knot returned, stabbing in her gut, as she tried to think how to respond. She glanced around, hoping someone would defend her. Stand up for all that she was trying to do. Flawed or not. She was the one up here speaking, not xem. Her eyes met Ador's. But . . . he wasn't an insider either. He seemed to be urging her on. Next to him, she saw Dayn's grimace, twisting with sadness. Luja, fists balled, and Tum, covering her mouth in horror.

She knew the flaws of their leaders. She'd been maimed by one, enduring the bullying of others. She'd left the Circles; she'd given it all away, and now *she* was the pro-government one? But that was her story. That wasn't their business to parse, or her burden to explain. She was learning too. And this pyr's words, they were the Violence, no matter how xe masked them. Dime was open to discuss if she was wrong, but not like this. Her gut wrenching, she tried to find words, not for this pyr or xyr squad, but for the others still listening. If someone was still listening.

"I'm not here to defend the Light. Or the High Seat. Or anyone or anything. I am here to say that fixing our wounds requires understanding of our shared situation. Our flaws. Our hope as well as our harm. And only each of us can examine that for ourselves. There are harmful pyrsi in the world, dominated by harmful actions. But there are more that want peace. But we are fragmented, scared." *Misinformed.* She stood straighter.

"I'm not scared anymore." This was . . . a lie. She corrected it. "No. I am scared. But I want to share what I've seen. To talk to pyrsi. To listen to what they've seen. To learn from each other. To propose that there are enough of us who care, that we could lead a better way. And we cannot march out there like a new band of Sol's Pillars—or Risers—with negativity and judgment as our banners."

She refused to look back at the pyr or xyr supporters around xem, but instead scanned the rest of the room. "Don't let pyrsi convince you that's the only way. I don't believe it. We must march under kindness. Beauty. *Compassion.* Yes, standing up for each other. Showing the world what can be, while still being honest about what is. Understanding it is complicated. Persisting anyway."

The pyrsi at the table were laughing. Dime reeled with confusion.

What had been an uncomfortable discussion, but at least a good start twice before, now had been tainted by this pyr's attack. It was an attack. Xe could have engaged in conversation, but xe'd chosen not to. Xyr toxicity, shrouded as justice, had taken what could have been a productive exchange, and turned it into harm itself. She felt alone in this huge room, an enemy of the cause she had thought they'd held in common. Maybe she should never have said anything.

Maybe she shouldn't be saying it now.

With a look at Dayn, Ador, and her children, she met each of their gazes. She remembered that they understood her, that they loved her, and she drew strength from those truths. And she tried again. "I am not here to defend or shelter any harm that has occurred or is occurring or will occur. I am not here to say that anyone should allow it to pass, or not speak it for what it is. I am not here to be *perfect*. I am here to say that we are a community, and we are stronger than those who seek to divide us."

"Maybe there's reasons to be divided," another pyr called.

"In some cases, sure, but not all of us. Not pyrsi at large. I mean, do you want the Great War to return?" Several pyrsi gasped. "No, really, is that our path? The Violence? Control? I know it's complicated, but I don't want that. Do you? We won't all agree, and sometimes our disagreements will have no easy resolution. Sometimes we will even believe others around us bring *harm*. That's why we have to work together. Why we have to keep talking. To each foster change, in the ways we are best able. To work for each of our freedom."

She rested a shaking hand over her heart. "That's what I propose—a banner of freedom. I'm like many of you. I've lived a long life feeling unable to be myself, in all my facets. This is wrong. It is wrong to ask anyone to live this way, so long as they are not proffering harm to others, as our society defines it."

A different pyr spoke up. "What if our society is wrong in that definition? Who draws that line between one pyr and another?"

She'd thought about that a lot. "No single pyr gets to draw that line. We find it, together. That's why we join the Free Winds. We join the Foundry. We speak. We discuss. We offer our voice. We live by our values. We learn and adjust. We talk to those who disagree. Not condone. Talk. Show compassion. Inform. And when enough of us stand together, then we will stand forever. But it is not easy. I am not here to tell you it is easy. I am here, offering my thoughts and proposing that it's time to speak. To no longer let our voices be ignored by those in power."

"What if those in power ignore us?"

"If there are enough of us who speak, then they will not be in power much longer."

Dime didn't know if she'd said all of it right. She didn't know why she had to, when she was here trying to do her best. Seeing the mix of reactions around her, she wanted to crawl back to the lounge and cry alone with a ferm. But that wouldn't help. Or maybe it would.

She was supposed to be taking questions, but her mind spun and she didn't think that she could. "I'll be at the party later," she forced herself to say. "If you want to talk further, let me know. As long as it's really a talk." She opened her hands outward. "I've been through a lot to get here, just as we all have. No subject would shock me now. Whatever it is, let me know. We'll discuss. And most importantly, thank you for your time. Thank you for listening."

The pyr in front rose in xyr seat. "She's trash. Look, she won't even—"

She would not engage this way. She would not be drawn in. Dime rushed from the room, hearing the calls behind her that she was garbage and a coward.

It took Dime a while to get into the swing of the party. Mostly, she feared that the one who had attacked her, or others who agreed with xem, might do so again. She couldn't shake the feeling of an open wound, one that felt worse than anything Sol's Pillars or even Neimano had inflicted on her. Ella had said it was the oppressors who would make her fear stepping forward, not allies. Yet, how simplistic would it be to think no one here was flawed, that everyone here held all her values, simply because they held some.

Trash. Garbage. No one should ever be called these things.

Dime knew others had faced such feelings for cycles. Uchitar, mocked for his troubles. Ella and Suzannelina, kept from their homes. Volana, limited by her class. Ador, looked down on as a pyr that had abandoned his. But Dime hadn't known she would be attacked for trying to help. She wished she were as strong as her friends.

She hadn't been prepared for it, and now she felt discarded. Lesser. But why should her own feelings matter, for such a small thing? Eventually, with Luja's whispered jokes and encouraging smiles, she managed to accept her child's offered arm and take in the scope of the event, though the weight of her distress continued to pull at her.

The large room had been dimmed, allowing pyrsi to immerse into color, companionship, and sound. A band was playing music from a corner of the room. The musical style was not familiar to her—mid-tempo, with ranged melodies layered over soft rhythms that kept strictly to the beat. Though the band had one soly on the stage, she presumed this was traditional music of the Heartland, at least the type designed for dancing.

The glowstones hanging from the ceiling had been modified to cast down different colors onto the dance area as pyrsi swirled and turned. Luja left to dance with a pyr around vis age, leaving Dime as alone as she felt. She sighed, looking to see where she could at least find the bar.

Then a petite figure, dressed in an exquisitely handsome suit, whisked past, offering his arms for a dance.

"Hi," she said to her friend.

"Hi?" Ador replied. "That's what I get?"

It was. She couldn't tell him how she felt, how his presence— his unconditional and unwavering friendship—flooded her with emotion. Instead, she allowed him to sweep her away. It was a one-sided sweep; Ador's elegant motions were entirely ruined in Dime's awkward lumber. Of course, Ador pretended he was dancing with the Light herself. Then, Dime remembered, he probably had. At least this made her relax a little.

"Change is hard, Dime. Do you see now, why the extremists get fuel? It is much easier to join a cause without nuance than to join a cause. It is much harder to unwind the details."

With some guilt, Dime remembered how many cycles Ador had been doing this same kind of work. Yet he was here, comforting her, when she had not been there to do the same.

"I feel like I messed everything up. I guess I shouldn't have just talked, without thinking through it more. I shouldn't have even come here, I guess. It was supposed to be a break, I mean, not a break. Anyway." Her words fell out. "Ella thought I'd find pyrsi here who would help."

"I think you did," he said. "Look how many pyrsi showed up for your talks."

They called me trash. "No one defended me."

Ador slowed a little. "I didn't want to fuel xem, when xe wasn't even trying to have a conversation. If I were up there with you, I would have said something to everyone. Hey. Pyrsi watching me now, they know where I stand." That last bit, he said with emphasis.

She tried to offer a grateful smile. Not having energy to say more, she let her friend glide her around the room, and tried to enjoy the joyful music and the changing colors of the space, shining out over the dark night.

"It's so nice here," she said with a sigh. "I would have enjoyed it a lot, I think, if I had kept my mouth shut."

"I know," he said, pulling her closer. "I know."

A familiar ma'pyr appeared between them. "I do believe you are dancing with my spouse."

"Oh, dear," Ador whispered. "He's jealous." Switching his hands over to reach for Dayn, Ador and Dayn danced around the floor, making fancy turns and swirls that eclipsed any of Dime's own efforts.

Her spirits lifted watching the two ma'pyrsi dancing together. Sometimes, it took remembering the pyrsi who did care, and not worrying so much about the ones who did not approach life with love. And the pyrsi who cared, they were her soul. Her freedom.

She thought how Rock would enjoy this place. A member of Dawn's Circle, Rock had spent cycles trying to understand the fairies, and here she could casually live among them. Maybe Rock would even dance. Maybe.

Dayn returned just then, his eyes alight. "As I was saying?" He offered her an arm.

"No fancy stuff."

"I know," he said, instead allowing them to drift, without fanfare, around the lit-up space, then finally escorting her to a bench. With his arm around her they sat in silence, watching the others celebrate.

"I admire you," he said.

Dime didn't want to be admired. She didn't want to be held to standards she simply couldn't meet. She just wanted happiness, for herself, her family, and for anyone else she could impact. And she wanted to feel they all deserved it. And, with that understanding, she held onto her spouse, and did her best to let it all go. For now. For a while.

Almost as if responding to a wish, she was surprised to see she hadn't noticed the bartender from before, who was there, running a towel through his hands. What was his name? She couldn't stay Underground forever, she knew. No, and she didn't want to. She understood, now, what Ella meant. But, while she was here, she might as well try that avian one more time.

The balance was perfection.

Interlude

Wanting to arrive early to the stage show, Timini was glad that the couple looked to be wrapping things up. They seemed to have forgotten he was there a take or so ago, but it would be rude to leave without saying goodbye. Besides, he needed his register signed.

So he sat on the far edge of the bed staring at the branches swaying outside the window across the room. A wing, he wasn't even sure which partner's wing, flipped over and smacked him in the arm, but neither of the involved parties seemed to notice.

"Mmmm," the fe'pyr cooed, and the couple settled down onto the wide mattress. Relieved, Timini stood and stepped over toward the washroom. He'd brought a nice robe for the show, not wanting to put his work clothes on again of course, but also because he felt like dressing up. It was supposed to be one of the best shows Pito had seen in a while.

Then, behind him, he heard a series of thumps and looked back to see the couple was fully engaged again. *All harm,* he grumbled. What was this, round three?

"Timini," the ma'pyr called.

He didn't have such a bad job. One of his good friends spent all shift scrubbing and restuffing upholsteries, and her shifts were longer spans. While ergosex was an optional role for obvious reasons—not everyone was extrasexual for starters—his family had a long, proud tradition of fostering some of the most requested ergosex experts in Pito.

Not sure what that was going to mean if he was late to the best show of the season. However, he took his reputation seriously, so, he hid his grumbles and stood tall, allowing the ma'pyr's full view of his widely-spread body to invite some arousal back into his system. The ma'pyr, noticing the change, beamed and beckoned him over. Taking inclusion seriously, Timini smiled at the fe'pyr as well, gauging her intent to participate.

A few takes later, with tired wings, he was glad to see his spouse and friends had saved him a spot in the busy clearing. He swept down onto his seat, folded his wings behind him, and plunked his bag under the bench. "Hurry, they're starting," his spouse whispered. "Glad you made it."

With a quick peck to her cheek, he settled down and watched with delight as the actors took the stage.

Act 3

EMERGENCE

Klein's welcoming smile held an otherworldly lilt, and Dime wondered what the pyr's story might be. His eyes twinkled like one who understood the soul of a pyr, though Dime had learned a long time before, there was only so good of friends one could ever realistically be with a bartender. This one, round-faced and with slight coloration to his slate cheeks, offered no details about himself, yet Dime had the sense that if she needed someone to talk to, he'd be there. His presence comforted her, with an inherent feeling that maybe he understood.

She wasn't sure how to thank a pyr for an inherent feeling, and so she simply thanked him for the drinks, but to herself she issued a quiet wish that she might see him again. After a last look back to acknowledge his wistful nod, Dime gingerly walked the two teetering drinks back to where Dayn sat.

"Come on, let's go over there," he said, pointing to a long table surrounded by mingling pyrsi.

She started to object.

"Trust me," he said.

Sighing, she took a sip of her drink and walked over to the table.

"Hey," a pyr said, moving over to make room. "I'm sorry about earlier. You wouldn't be here if you weren't trying to help. Most of us know that."

"It's a really great place," another added. "Pyrsi can be tense, but we know that being awful to other pyrsi doesn't help anyone. Here, have a seat?"

Inside, it frustrated her that the insults had been so public, but the support remained so private. She was at least glad for the friendly faces. Hiding the knot of fear she still carried, she tried to smile back. "Thank you," she said. "It's fascinating here, and I really appreciate your hospitality."

"We'll tell you more, if you'd like."

"I'd love that." Dime scooted in, and soon, with her drink, was resting on a tall chair. Dayn sat close to one side, blocking the view of her legs, which dangled above the floor. He rested his hand on her knee, and it felt nice. She patted it back.

Half-expecting tales of melancholy, she was instead delighted as each pyr around the table told anecdotes. Friends they'd met, events they'd hosted. Mishaps and holidays and all the little moments that made a place a home.

Though glad to be together here with her family and friends, Dime missed having a home. She kept that thought to herself.

After a long rest and an extra cup of brew, Dime was surprised by a knock at the door. Dayn and Tum had gone to find what was rumored to be a fully-stocked building shop, and she didn't expect them back for a while. Maybe it was Luja. Or, perhaps, Volana.

"Come in," she said, setting down her notebook. She'd been brainstorming ideas of how to better formalize a coalition. Determined, she'd been pushing herself to write whatever thoughts, however silly, came to mind—that trick usually coaxed out something worthwhile. So far, she hadn't come to any conclusions she felt good about.

As the door opened, Dime felt more than a little embarrassed to see Hin, Ador's younger assistant in the Free Winds, peering nervously into the room. Embarrassed because she'd essentially forgotten that he was there with them. Her mind felt so scattered.

"Please, come in," she urged. "It's so good to see you again."

He stepped inside, pulling the door shut behind him and stopping to scratch the ears that Agni offered. "It's always good to see you."

She was glad, by the casual greeting, that he seemed to have settled in some. He'd been a fan of hers before, for rebelling against the Circles, as he saw it. She wondered what the advocate had heard about her talks.

Hin stood up. "Everything well? You know, in this place?"

Dime didn't know how to answer that, but she managed a stiff nod.

"Yeah. I know. So, I was wondering if Luja was here. Ador mentioned ve was around."

"Ve is," Dime said. "But ve has vis own room, next door. Here, I haven't had a chance to talk to you. Please, sit down." With a jolt, Dime had the sudden realization that the pyr might not have been looking for table talk with a Gamh many cycles his elder when his friend was next door, but she'd committed now. Anyway, it would be good for him to talk to someone in what, with his background, had to be a jarring place to learn existed; Dime could see how he was doing. Ador saw potential in the younger pyr, and had seemed concerned about him.

Or, really, with the time she'd had here, it didn't feel so great being alone in the room, and the friendly face brought comfort. She'd try and keep it short.

"What do you think?" she asked, as Hin joined her at the table. "I know you were uncertain about the fairies before, but you've had a chance to meet some here?"

He squirmed in his seat. "Not much. Ador writes up his notes, and they're all scratched out. I've been lettering them properly for him, so we can share them with the Free Winds, back in the city. Keeps me busy. Besides, it seems like a big party here. Don't see the point."

Dime felt similar, except in her case, it was a party that didn't really want her there. Yet, Hin looked agitated and cramped. It'd do him good to get out some. "Any town seems like a party if you only visit its hub. The complex is huge. Lives being lived, all the way between Sol's Reach and the Heartland. Literally! It seems like you're missing a good opportunity here," she added, realizing how parental she sounded as the words came out. She kept on, though. "I think when you get to know the fairies, you'll see we're all more similar than you'd think. They have a different culture, different thought processes sometimes, but the same hopes and fears. I mean, you're here. Why not get out and at least talk to pyrsi?"

Hin sighed, running his hand across the tabletop. "I just don't know why it had to go this way. The Free Winds was about changing our government, about getting rid of repressive laws and customs that tell pyrsi who they're supposed to be. The nonsense I dealt with back in my hometown. Hemsa and high-class control, and the harmed off Sol's Pillars. It wasn't supposed to be about fairies. I mean, you know that. You resisted the Circles. That's how this all started, right? And then the fairies had to intervene. I mean, you were there! And I admire you for how you resisted the fairies right from the start, but ever since then, it seems like that's the focus. *Fairies. Not us.*"

"Well." She thought about how to word this. "I agree that there were other issues on our mind, both when I left the Circles and when you joined the Free Winds. Yet, the broader issue was forced then, wasn't it? And you can't imagine Lodon just going back to pretending that didn't happen." Every time she said something like this, the clear image of Neimano and his guards, back in her home, flashed into her view like a master painting. It felt etched into her memory, not fading with the turns. She tried to gather herself.

"And I've had time, now, to think about it—we all have—and I've concluded we shouldn't go back. Those boundaries were harming pyrsi, we just didn't see it. Or even, we were kept from seeing it, back to your original point. Anyway. Ada-ji needs to be united. That's my view."

"Yeah," he muttered. "I just don't know."

Dime was glad he was thinking through it, and not just setting his mind. Though, like she'd said, he needed to get out of his room, if that's where he'd been holed up. He really could use some socialization, whether with fairies or not. Of course, Dime had just spent the last bell or so considering hiding in the bedroom and never leaving again. Who was she to judge?

"Hey, I sort of understand." She set her elbows onto the table.

"You do?" He perked up.

"Well, yes. I'm not sure if you heard, but I gave some public talks, in addition to conversations I've had."

"I only heard a little from Ador," he admitted. "I've—" He stared off at the wall.

"They didn't go well. At least the last one didn't. After a bell or two here, I'd been filled with hope. That this place was the perfect example. It proved pyrsi could find a way to live together and promote peace and understanding, even when they shared different cultures and values. Then—" She tried to find the words, but she didn't want to tell him what happened. It was still too raw, and she didn't want to give fuel to his prejudices.

"I suppose I'm just saying I understand how it feels when the world is not how you thought it would be. What it's like to feel upended. Could I ask you to consider that?"

Another knock sounded at the door.

"Come in," Dime said, as Luja whipped into the room.

"Oh," ve blurted, seeing Hin at the table. "Hin! Hey! Game buddy—been a while. Guess you're cool with fairies now?"

Hin struggled to react, then said, "I'm here, right? Do you . . . do you want to go talk?" He stood up, stepping toward the door.

Luja put vis hands on either side of vis waist. "Oh, I'm going to stay here a while. Visiting my mother." Ve pointed at Dime. "You're welcome to stay too." Ve swung a chair to the table, as if leaving Hin's available.

Hin stayed standing, not turning fully back around. "That sounds great, but I need to get back. Well. Good to talk to you both."

"Anytime, Hin." Dime waved as he walked out and closed the door. Knowing an avoidance when she saw one, she wondered if there were questions she ought to be asking her child. But a look at vis face and she had the sense it was better to let it drop. She'd talk about Hin later with Ador. Maybe see if there was something else she could do.

"Know what I think?" Luja asked.

Dime wasn't sure if this was about Hin. "No, what?"

"A long time ago, we ran from our power. There's probably a reason why, and it's probably long lost. But we built our city as far from the diamonds as we could. And then we buried all of it. We just . . . had to know. There's no way we didn't know. The fairies, though, they embraced it. They built their city next to it. They allowed it to thrive."

Trying to catch up with her child's sudden exploit into cultural proximity to the diamond caves, she considered Luja's theories. "What if it's the opposite?" she finally asked. "What if we built our cities without knowing? Or . . . what if we built them where the resources lay? The fairies at the heart of the forest and the solies at the base of the mountains? What if they just were lucky?"

Luja squinted. "I . . . well maybe. But either way, we aren't more or less powerful than anyone else. We hid our power, and it hid inside us. Ma-ma, I have wings." Ve reached a hand to pat over vis back. "They're just inside!"

Maybe it was too many bells, too many turns now, of feeling isolated, but the first thought that came to mind was again that Dime had never been given that choice. At first, she didn't have wings. But neither did everyone she knew. Now, they all had that power. Everyone except Dime. But . . . her hand stretched up to her chest. She had her pendant. Given to her, per her theory, by the same pyr that had taken the same power away from her. She could feel, not directly, but in her mind, the two scars on her back where her wings would have been.

Noting Luja's wide eyes, brimming with hope and curiosity,

Dime could not take a stride of this away from ver. She wouldn't. "You do. You really do. Now," she winked, "what are you going to do with them?"

Luja hopped up from the seat. Giving vis mother a quick, almost air kiss, ve popped out from the room, leaving as abruptly as ve'd entered.

And again, Dime sat there alone. She'd been alone before. On the plains. In the forest. Even up in the old woods. And now, here, in a cave connecting the two lands. Not the first cave, she remembered. But before, Rock had been with her. Her gaze turned up to Rock's carved owl on the shelf.

She still had no idea if Rock had really made it for her or if she'd been being her usual sarcastic self. She didn't care. The owl was exceptionally carved. It wasn't the bird, or the size, or even the skill of the carving. The eyes of the bird almost came alive, like something that wanted more, but didn't know where to find it. And so the owl was watching.

For a single piece of wood, carved with a prison blade, it was stunning in its beauty.

She tried to remember why they'd fought. Rock had felt she'd been too open with Intinpalo, she supposed. It just didn't seem like that big of a deal. But, then, before that. They'd argued over other things, like Rock talking to Olok without her permission.

Rock didn't think she needed permission from Dime.

And she didn't, about things that affected her. But the Project Diamondsong victims . . . they weren't in Rock's lane. Dime was right about that.

Being right didn't fix that feeling she'd had ever since the forest.

Though. What would have happened if Rock had been there when Neimano attacked? Would she have been hurt? Would Stern Eyes not have used her valence? She had no idea.

Rock shouldn't have talked to Olok. But maybe she was right about something. Why shouldn't Olok be at least offered the opportunity to discuss, or to help? It really wasn't fair to say Olok should chase after Dime when Dime couldn't find herself half the turns.

Though Dime's knot did not subside, something clicked into place. Dime needed to talk to Olok too.

And maybe some bells away from all this would cure her doubt and fear—or distract her from it. She didn't know. It was all muddled. She felt muddled. If Ella had thought this place would clarify her thoughts, it hadn't. They were static, like the charge before a storm. Heavy, like the rain that didn't have a place yet to fall.

Yes. She was going to talk to Olok. At least give her that choice.

A while later, when Dayn and Tum had returned, she asked Dayn what he thought. Sort of.

"There's someone in the city I want to talk to."

"Alright?" Dayn seemed to think there was more. There really wasn't more.

"Someone who . . . may be like me. Who knows. I just want to check in."

"Whatever you need to do. Will you be . . . safe . . . in the city?"

She was about the same amount of safe anywhere, she realized. Here, she'd thought she was safe. And look what happened. Lodon. That was home. And she still hoped, whatever they said here, the Circles might begin to listen. Or be made to listen. Either way. If peace could be found, she wasn't going to turn anyone away who might be convinced to help bring it. And no matter what one thought of the Circles, they were still comprised of individual pyrsi. With a wide variety of views, once freed from not expressing them.

"It irritates me," she said, suddenly realizing what Hin had said that bothered her the most, "that pyrsi think I rebelled against the Circles by leaving them."

Dayn nodded, reaching out to offer her a hand. She took it.

"I rebelled the whole time I was there. I pushed for change. I took stands. I helped pyrsi when I could. I rebelled the whole harmed time." She paused, finding herself out of breath. "I left when I realized it wasn't working. That I didn't have the leverage I needed from there, in the inside, and I couldn't support a system that would take me to where I would. I may have made a statement by leaving. But it was an empty statement. One that helped no one.

"The rebelling? That's what I tried to do all along." She glanced away from her spouse. "And I failed."

"I'm glad you left," he murmured. "And if you need to see someone, then go. It's fine. We'll be here."

Last time he'd said that, they'd all raced off to live with the newts. But it was certainly more comfortable here. And it's not as if they were going to walk the width of Ada-ji when Dime could provide them transport.

"Ok. I'll come back." She almost added "soon," but then if she were delayed, they'd worry.

Dayn moved closer. "I don't know if it needs to be right away, but . . . could I ask you on a date?"

"What?" Dime thought she had heard.

"A date. My spouse. I love you. I love you a lot. More than that worry does. Let's go out to one of the lounges. No, let's go sit on one of the patios. And enjoy the view. And just . . . not worry for a bell or two."

A few takes later, she and Dayn were seated out on a small patio, looking over the ravine with a basket full of root crisps. Dime scooted toward him, settling against the warmth of his arm. "I love you." It wasn't that she could stop worrying, but here, just for a little bit, she could kind of pretend. She set it all aside, letting the ache dim a bit.

"I love you, and our family, more than anything on Ada-ji." Dayn squeezed her hand.

Feeling, in that moment, that Ada-ji consisted only of that one, wonderful pyr, she leaned in and surrendered to feeling nothing but Dayn's closeness.

The kids hadn't even questioned her departure, both agreeing it might be good for her to get away for a while. They'd felt like her parent, not the reverse, as they'd shuffled around, helping her pack and wrapping little snacks and folded notes for her journey. "This is a surprise," one read, in Tum's tilted handwriting. "Open later."

Volana had offered her a quick hug and promised she'd see her soon. Dime had asked Ador if he had any messages for Batu, and he'd said no, but thanked her for the consideration. "Be well," he'd added, with a brush to her cheek.

Thus Dime stood in the hallway, all packed up, and arguing with a twinge of doubt about what she was doing. She said she'd been ready to go, so what would she do now—go back? Dime took a breath.

Remembering that Bown had asked the courtesy of a conversation before anyone left for the outside, she went to find ver. Not finding ver in vis office, she was directed to check a workroom, and also a storage area that was being cleaned. Then, she ran into ver in a corridor.

"Bown," she said, as ve made to walk past.

Ve turned back.

"I need to visit the city for a while. Lodon. I understand the secrecy, and I'll be back soon."

Facial expressions were harder to read under all that blue-dyed facial hair, but she could definitely see a scrunching of concern. Ve opened vis mouth, hesitating.

"Is there an issue?"

"We're cautious about pyrsi leaving."

She wasn't sure where ve was going with this. Certainly they wouldn't hold her here. Actually, she wasn't going to find out.

"Burge Bown. I need to leave for a bit. I promise you I will hold the rules of the Underground sacred to the very best of my ability. Any decisions on your future will be made by the citizens of this place. Not by me. I consider myself a visitor," she clarified.

"Now, should I find my way back to the entrance, or would

someone be able to help me work the door? I would prefer the help, as I know the use of valence is sensitive." She cringed, realizing that sounded more threatening than she'd intended. But, really, when a pyr said they wanted to leave, that should generally be afforded. Dime waited as Bown stood there, hands clasped together.

"You've changed this place," ve finally said. "I can feel it. Please understand that many of us have mixed emotions about that."

Dime remembered what Ador had said about Bown. That ve wanted a better, more open world. But ve'd been here a long time. "I understand," was all she said.

The walk back to her chair restored her spirits a great deal. Sol shone down from overhead, and birds swept by, returning, she was sure, to the forest beyond the cliff. The open breeze invigorated her, and she was almost sorry when she caught view of their little wooden platform behind the natural stone pillars, her chair waiting atop it. With a final glance in the direction of the hidden city, she sat down and lifted up into the sky.

Dime had never traveled to Lodon from this far eas, and after a while of traversing the vast, rocky plains, she enjoyed gazing downward as the surcity corridor came into view. She'd never actually seen the lower villages before, a spattering of tight-knit communities. With cultures based around one place, they tended to be lived in by those who had always lived there, and not visited by those who hadn't. Travelers found little reason to traverse their low hills—without the larger towns or the rugged appeal of the central and wesside plains, or the outlaw villages that tended to sprawl further norwes, the lower surcity wasn't of much interest to adventurers. Even the IC stayed out, for the most part. Dime peered down with interest, wondering if anyone noticed her shape, passing high above.

Then the hills rose to steeper ridges and the mountains grew distant across the ravine, and the sections most pyrsi were used to spread below her. Closer to Lodon, the surcity corridor was known for its series of small communities dedicated to cultivating food supplies. A pattern of valleys rippled against the towering peaks of deep gullies, rich with small, winding farms. While the towns themselves kept fairly private, there were some spots among the steep hills that hosted aging or distilling fermenteries—both fruit and grain based. These catered to the wealthy and upper class of nor Lodon, for whom the reasonable trip sur provided some variety.

Dime watched the valleys pass by and occasionally turned to enjoy the mountains over the ravine to her right. The fissure widened and grew more severe, into the broadening gulch that bordered Lodon's eas wall.

While normally the sight of the towers brought a rush of yearning, today they did not, as the scenery flying nor had provided her a brief respite, and she worried a little, what she might encounter here. She continued to fly up, over the gulch, not even wanting to see whether there were still crowds at the gates. They weren't the focus of her energy, even if she had energy for them.

Yet she wasn't willing to risk losing the makeshift chair that Ella had scrapped together, and so she landed out of sight of the medical enclave where Rock had said Olok worked, hiding the chair within a patch of trees.

The audacity of the moment struck her abruptly when, after growing used to the individualism of the Underground, she realized she was walking into a renowned medical enclave with a fully-visible head of white hair. Well. They'd deal with it.

She walked up to the front desk, as the clerk there gasped. "Yes, hello." She thought about asking for Olok, but considered that would betray the medic as somehow associated with her. "I'm meeting someone upstairs." She pointed up. Then, with as much confidence as she could convey, she marched on past, right toward a back staircase, hoping there'd be a directory. At least if Olok was out, she'd know where to go.

"Wait," the clerk uttered. "Burge."

Dime stopped. She wasn't looking for a confrontation either. She turned back around and offered an easy smile. "Yes, is it alright for me to go now?"

The clerk opened and closed xyr mouth, glancing from side-to-side as if hoping someone else would enter.

Someone did.

"Yes, I saw her too, from the window. I'll take care of it. Don't be afraid. I'll do what needs done and keep you out of it." A pyr dressed in medic wraps turned to Dime and spoke in a firm voice. "Please. Come with me. Now."

The clerk's exhale was audible, as xe seemed to shrink back into the area behind the desk.

Recognizing the serious, but not harmful, tone, Dime did what the pyr said and followed xem out. They walked what seemed a back way through the enclave, past the bucketpull shaft and around a staircase, until suddenly the medic opened a door and urged Dime through. The door clicked behind them, in a small room with a center table, and a side cart upon which rested empty serving dishes and a brew carafe.

"I asked her to leave me alone," the pyr growled. "And now you!"

Dime realized, then, this must be Olok. "Yes, I'm sorry about that. Rock, my friend, well. I asked her not to talk to you. She did anyway."

"She seemed nice." Sighing, Olok sat at the table, gesturing for Dime to join her. "And that doesn't explain your visit. Fe'Olok." She fanned her fingers. "I presume you are Fe'Dime?"

Dime nodded, taking the offered seat. "I'm sorry for the circumstance, and I really am sorry to bother you."

"Then why are you?"

"I'd say I'm here to offer you an apology, but that's just selfish reasoning, since I feel bad about being here, but I'm clearly here."

At least Olok smiled at that.

"It's hard to explain. I felt . . . drawn to visit. I guess, knowing you already know, and knowing that just talking to me won't change that, I just wanted to say hi once. To confirm that it's true, and you're not alone. To offer you any of the answers that I've learned. Or not. Anyway, hi."

The medic crossed her arms over her wraps and sighed. "The hair."

"I know. It just sort of happened, but now I'm feeling stubborn. It shouldn't be such a big deal."

"Of course it shouldn't. But it is. And, look, Dime, I've got a good life here helping pyrsi adapt, heal, and cope. What good does it do if I can't do that anymore?"

"No, I know. I don't want that for you either. I won't come back, ok. I just . . . wanted to tell you that you don't have to worry about me. And Rock won't say anything either. I know her. She won't."

Olok drummed her fingers silently on the table, seeming to think. "So since you're here, I'm curious. Who else do you know?"

It was clear from her tone, she didn't mean in general. She meant Neimano's victims.

"I have talked to two others." Dime wasn't sure she should reveal them, and wondered why Olok, who seemed thoughtful and considerate, would ask. "One is troubled. Stays in his home and either does not speak, or cannot. The other is a pyr of wealth. Lives a good life, it seems. Almost tried to follow me around. But. Well. That was too much."

"Kolk," Olok said.

Dime nodded. Yes, Kolk was the first of the two.

"He's deeply affected by what he's been through. The realization that we hold something"—Dime knew she meant valence—"that is said to be inherently wicked is not an easy thing for a ch'pyr to grasp. Not when xe has no one to tell. No one to explain."

"Yeah, I suppose I was lucky. I didn't know." Dime knew this was because the diamond pendant had been absorbing her energy, keeping it from manifesting as valence. "I really only just found out. Only a few turns ago." It had been thirteen since her first escape, yet only three since the caves. "When they showed up at my home, I didn't even know then."

"I don't know the other one you mentioned, and I'm not asking. I'm glad, though, that xe seems well."

Dime knew she was referring to Nafat, the museum curator who'd almost seemed excited at the news. "He may not be. But, yes, he is a very open pyr. Perhaps that kept the . . . power from manifesting. I had to tell him." Seeing Olok's squint, she hastened to clarify. "I didn't need to tell you once Rock surmised it, because I knew you were aware. You had to be. You know, the incident." Olok grimaced. Rock had told her about it; an odd case that now seemed entirely explained by Olok's use of fairy valence to save a ch'pyr.

"Those who didn't know, I feared . . . the pyr who did this would come after them. That they wouldn't know to protect themselves." Dime hoped Olok understood.

"The pyr. Please. I don't want to know xem. Or xyr name. But, just, xe is a fairy?"

"Yes. A fairy. Someone who is dangerous even now."

Head bent, Olok muttered, "I suppose I'd hoped—"

"I understand," Dime said. She did. No one would wish a pyr ill, but they might feel better thinking xe wasn't still around. That their tragedy was some unfortunate incident of an era past, not a sickness that manifested even now. She understood. And if Olok didn't want to know Neimano's identity, she wouldn't tell her. That was her choice.

The air between them shifted with discomfort. She wondered why she was here. Whether this was what she had needed, why she'd flown all the way back. Either way, time to leave this pyr to her life. Maybe it was a mistake. Maybe it was necessary. Dime just couldn't keep second-guessing everything. So, she'd just leave.

"Here. You need to know." Olok reached out her hand, holding a flyer, printed hastily with a broad, single-color stamp. On it, there was a crude depiction of Dime's face, her hair, and her tattoos. Underneath were three lines of text, written in what Dime recognized as a Fo-ror style lettering:

THE ESCAPED AGENT FE'DIAMOND HAS VALENCE

She has Committed the Violence

Protect Your Families and Report to Authorities on Sight

Dime took the paper, trying to keep it steady in her hands. "Wow." *Did Neimano do this?* There was really no end to the pyr being a jerk.

"I'm sorry," Olok said. "Now, please . . . promise me you won't visit Kolk again."

"I won't." They both stood, uncomfortable, as Dime raised her head from the paper. "Is there anything you want to know from me? Before I go?"

Olok glanced away. "I know it sounds strange, but no. I've made my own way, these cycles. I've found a path. Dime. I'll be watching you out there. I don't believe this," she shook a finger at the paper. "Yet our paths are separate. I wish you the best. My role is here. Maybe yours . . . is out there."

Dime wasn't sure it was her role. And the knot inside her wasn't either. But Olok didn't need her burdens also. "Um. This is more for me than you, but may I at least offer a hug?" Dime felt a deep connection to this pyr, to someone she could never befriend, who would only see their own pain in her presence. And she hoped, maybe, she could at least convey that connection. Before they parted. But if not, she'd—

Rising slowly, Olok extended her arms. And just like a medic comforting a ch'pyr, she rubbed her hands across Dime's scarred back, separated only by the soft fabric of her shirt. "It's ok," she whispered. "It's not your fault."

Dime held close a stride longer, then stepped away. She knew her time here was done. "I'll leave the same way we walked," she said. "I'll get out right away. Olok. It was nice to meet you. I won't bother you again. But my door, when I get one, is always open to you. Live in peace."

Dime turned and reached for the door handle.

"Wait."

Dime turned back, her hand still extended.

"Jaza is another one. You didn't mention her, and I thought you should know. Now. I wish you well."

There was no need to question this information, or ask how she knew. There was certainty in the medic's eyes, and Dime would need time to understand what this meant. Jaza, the leader of Sol's Pillars. The group who had spread the most fear of the distant fairies, the fe'pyr who'd looked at her with disgust. Who'd shown no empathy for her plight, nor her children. *No.* She'd think about this later.

Olok stepped past Dime, opening the door. "Give me a few strides to clear the lobby."

"Thank you," Dime mouthed, then waited, nervous in the shadows of the hallway. Soon after, she was back outside, first in Sol's light, and then moving in the shadows between the petite, pruned trees.

Standing and listening to the sounds of the city, the calling of pyrsi and the grinding of toothcars along the busy road, Dime closed her eyes. Perhaps she should visit Jaza. What would it do? Did this news matter? She wasn't sure that it did.

She'd said she would return to the others, and so she would. But first, there was another stop to make.

Yorm did not disguise her fear when she saw Dime's face at her door. "I know about the flyers," Dime said. Yorm nodded.

Unsettled, she started to explain that she would leave, but Yorm raised a silencing hand. "He'd never forgive me." She followed the silent fe'pyr down the dark wood-paneled hallway, with a soft shag carpet and decorated only with a painting of each of Yorm and Zael's children.

Zael was not better.

The last time she'd seen him, he'd looked a little under, as her father might have said. Now, with a pained expression and blueish blotches under his eyes, he rested back on a swath of pillows, surrounded by glasses of liquid he'd not consumed, half-eaten snacks. A book rested in his lap, not even held in his hands, but propped open with a pair of smooth wooden shoe-horns. Sol's light streamed in from the window. "Dime!"

There was no awkwardness from Yorm's presence, for she tapped the door shut behind her, leaving them alone.

"You haven't saved it all yet," he said, smiling.

Dime snorted. "Turns out that's not so easy when you have a whole world of pyrsi, each moving their own way."

"The pyrsi who see it that way are the ones that we need. You'll get there."

"I'm dangerous, though." She held out the flyer. By his wide eyes, it was clear Yorm had not shown it to him. And she was still waiting for him to comment on her hair.

"Look at you!" His head snapped up, with more vigor than he'd had a stride past. "Do you really have valence?"

"I do. I was born there, in the Heartland. I had no idea." She shrugged. "But the rest of it, no." The part about the Violence was arguable, but she wasn't going to burden Zael with Neimano's misrepresentation.

His laughter was cut short by a cruel bout of coughing. Dime sat by, feeling helpless. She took her pendant necklace out and flipped it over her shirt. "It's powerful, too. Because of this pendant. I've always had it. I didn't tell pyrsi. Never wanted to show off, I suppose." It was more than that.

"That's beautiful." He seemed transfixed by the pendant, finally wrenching his gaze away.

"I don't want it," she said. "I tried to ditch it a while back, but a friend talked me into keeping it." *Yeah, Rock. Who left.* "The way it amplifies valence is tuned to me specifically, because I wore it for so long. I feel guilty about that. It's not mine. None of this is mine."

"The stone seems to think otherwise." After his burst of energy,

Zael appeared to deflate against the bed. "There's so much I want to talk to you about."

"I can stay," she said. "For a while."

Zael smiled, less than before. "I don't stay awake the same now. Besides, I guarantee Yorm has seen that flyer. She's probably sweating rivers right now." His eyes flicked, as with humor. "No, friend, my time has passed. But . . . it means so much that you're here. That I can see you one more time." He tried to sit up more, but just shifted a touch. "Nothing is more important . . . than your friends."

"All the work you did was important. All the ways you helped pyrsi."

He shook his head, just a little. "I couldn't have done any of it without my friends. The friends matter most." The corner of his mouth turned. "And you, in such danger! Yet you take time and risk to see an old scholar."

He wasn't old. That was the worst of it. But she wasn't here to argue. And Zael *was* a scholar. He loved the game of hypothesis more than anyone she'd ever met. She wanted to sit here and go over all of it with him. Get his theories, debate them. Yet she could see him tiring already. His eyes drooping. She tried to think of something she could leave him with. Something to consider.

The first idea that came to mind was Ja-lal valence. This was still such a new idea to her, that she would love—*love*—to hear what he thought. Whether he'd seen it, or whether the idea clicked now, the way she had seen it in Ella's eyes.

But she remembered her last visit here. His frustration at pyrsi telling him to heal from within, from placing a burden on him that should not be his to bear. Whatever he held inside him, he already knew.

Something else, then. There must be something.

"Oh! I have a secret for you. It's a really big secret." She wondered why her tone was changing, but there was something in his reaction that showed, while he'd pulled together at her entrance, it had been an effort. "The newts. I've met them. They are wonderful, and caring, and have an entire culture of their own. They have valence too. It's based on their emotion. You can feel their love or even their worry."

Heartened by Zael's muted excitement, Dime spoke a little longer, pausing once as the bells rang out through the city. She described their scales and feathers, the way that Juni placed sprigs into her shoulders to look fancy, and the way she placed trinkets into her burrow. She saw his fingers lift.

"I'm falling asleep," he murmured. "I'm sorry. I love you, friend."

"I love you, too." She saw him slumping over, and she took the pillow and tucked it tighter, to keep his head in place. Something caught her eye. His hemsa, the little tattoo that had marked him for a crime when he was young. A crime that was not pleasant, but the misstep of youth, long-ago superseded by his cycles of hard work and kind spirit.

Rising, she went to the door and called gently for Yorm. They stepped into the hallway. "Do you have some paint? For his skin?"

Yorm's lips held tight, and Dime realized she'd gone too far. So she was entirely surprised when, without words, Yorm returned with a small jar.

Back inside the room, with Yorm staying in the doorway, Dime held the jar in front of her friend. "Could I remove that hemsa, please? Just for me. It irritates me." Though she hoped he appreciated her attempt at humor, she did not want him to carry this anymore.

Too tired to speak, his eyes lit up, and Dime knew he had agreed. She leaned forward, and he rose a little to try and meet her, but his neck was too weak. Gently, she dabbed her finger into the paint, and over the tiny mark. As drawing was never her skill, she went back to her go-to doodle. A little wildflower with wispy petals. It wasn't much, but she knew Yorm wanted her to leave, and she'd pushed far enough.

Sweeping past the clutter, she reached quickly for a mirror on his bedstand, and lifted it before him.

A broad smile broke across his face. He lifted his hand, as if toward Yorm, and whispered. "Keep it."

Yorm rushed to his side, cradling his hand. "I will. I promise," she whispered back. Then she stood, walking into the hall. "It's time to go, Dime."

She nodded, glad Yorm was at least willing to give them one more moment. Looking at Zael's tired eyes, she had a thought. While she wouldn't place any burden on him, maybe the diamond could help. She really didn't need it. Her power was in her heart. She knew that now.

And so, she removed the pendant, setting it down onto Zael's chest, over his heart. Whatever it might do, he deserved it more than she.

She wanted to whisper something profound, but, choked up, she simply squeezed his hand, then stood, turning to see Yorm again in the doorway, her arms folded.

"Thank you," she whispered. She steadied herself against the tall bed. "Thank you. No one saw me. I'll be gone now. And Dayn, he is well too. And our children. If Zael asks."

Yorm's countenance broke a little at the mention of the others, but she did not respond. Dime left on her own, walking cautiously down the flights of stairs.

Glancing to ensure no one was in the tower lobby or near its entrance, Dime darted out, running until, if someone did see her, there would be no correlation to where she'd been. And then, feeling just as powerful as when she'd had the stone—for she no longer needed it—she grabbed a wide, chipped shingle that had been tossed into a corner of a building. Sitting on it while grasping each side tightly, she willed it away, flying through the air as below her, pyrsi gasped and pointed.

Landing abruptly in between the trees, she wasted no time strapping into her chair and lifting upward, accelerating away until Lodon was again a speck in the distance.

Only then did she cry.

The door to the Underground could not be opened from the outside, even with any standard amount of valence, but Bown had showed her where to stand until someone came to open it. "We'll see you," ve'd said.

And so Dime stood there, feeling as awkward as when her teacher had convinced her to sell give-back cookies, until the door clicked open before her. It wasn't Bown this time at the door, but a younger pyr who was friendly enough, and let her off on her way without too much hassle.

As she walked into Central, she again marveled at the view the daylight provided over the edge of their land. Almost expecting some sort of riot as she entered, she was relieved, this time, that even the pyrsi who noted her let her pass, uninterrupted. Ador had mentioned that the pyrsi here did not favor disruption, yet it was as if nothing had happened. Not that Dime believed that.

As she wound through the common space, she saw none of her family or friends, and so she headed back to their suite to see if anyone was there. She hoped they were. The events of the city still weighing on her mind, Dime wasn't in a mood to search the complex.

She tapped at the door. It was their private suite, but still feeling a visitor in this place, it felt more appropriate than the normal. "It's me." Hearing Dayn's voice, she eased open the door. Dayn welcomed her into a hug as he moved to meet her. Ador, sitting at the table, fanned his fingers, and Dime, really glad to see their friendly faces, walked over. Dayn returned to his seat across from Ador.

"I saw Zael," she said, resting her hands on the back of a chair. "I doubt he is long for the world."

Dayn bowed his head.

"I'm sorry," Ador said, his voice soft. "Your friend?"

Dime nodded. "He wouldn't want us to go on about it."

"If you ever need to talk," Ador offered, with a look to each of them.

"I know," Dime said. "Thanks." She drew a steadying breath. "Kids?"

"Out." Dayn raised his head, gesturing for Dime to sit. "Luja doesn't offer me vis itinerary, and I've stopped worrying about it. Tum loves the maker shop; she's there now helping to craft new tables for one of the playrooms." Dayn sighed.

"What?"

"I won't know what to do if our child follows me into the Construction Circle."

Dime laughed. "Don't worry. She's too independent."

"With two parents who were in the Circles?"

"I agree with Dime," Ador interjected. "You need not fear that your beautiful child will fall into your traps of despair."

"Thanks, Ador." She sat down and let out a huge breath. It turned out much more dramatic than she intended.

"Speaking of which?" Dayn tried to offer a helpful grin.

Reaching into her left side pocket, she pulled out the copy of the flyer that Olok had given her. With a plunk as dramatic as her sigh, because why not go with it, she unfolded it onto the table.

Honestly, she did not appreciate the hoots and cheers that followed from what was supposed to be her pep squad. With nothing really to say about that, she soft-glared back and forth between them.

"Look, I'm sorry," Ador started. "But if you were truly upset by this, you wouldn't have announced it to us with quite as much flair. I mean, it's a terrible thing, to expose your information without your consent. But you *know* how we feel about that. You do! But, look, we're seeing something entirely encouraging."

"This hair?" she offered, rustling it with her fingers.

"This Seat, the one who did this to you, *you have him scared.*"

Staring down at the paper, she supposed that was true. Neimano had seemed intent on keeping the secret. He'd let her leave the complex, even, knowing what risk he'd bear if she used valence right in front of the crowd. And Ador had recognized the fairy-style lettering too; he must have drawn the same conclusion she did, that Neimano had made the flyers.

But. That was in the Heartland. With the current state of things, it was fairly assured that any common folk of the Heartland wouldn't be flying around Lodon to see the flyers. In fact, she realized, Neimano hadn't either. These pyrsi he'd hired, he probably just dropped them off with them and told them to paste them around. *Gross.*

"Hey," Dayn said, softening his tone. "We know this is hard. Aren't we here? We lost our home. We lost our security. Our children have witnessed the Violence, now, at least twice. I know it's hard. But here, in private, can't we just say that you're awesome? You know, like Tum says?"

"I suppose," she grumbled. "It's more than that, though. I'm not here to admire my own pity. Or guilt. Or whatever. It's more the larger question. Every new turn, I'm like, alright! Time to act! I didn't start this, but I'm in it now. But why? Why any of it? Why am I starting over, making things worse, and what if I'm not the right pyr all along? Why do I remain out front of all this, when all I wanted to do was open a music school?

"I mean, I know. I know that's flawed. It's all flawed. And so, since I can't think about it, or say it perfectly, I need to just go back into my chair and try again and fly around with a muddled identity and make pyrsi uncomfortable." She slumped back into her seat.

Ador's face drew with concern as Dayn sat forward. "I agree. You're not as special as pyrsi want you to be. Pyrsi want perfect heroes, not real pyrsi who try to navigate a complicated world. We all have pitfalls and opportunities. Sometimes big. Sometimes small. You're just aware of and leaning into yours. And, ok, I agree, yours happen to be a bit big right now. But," he made sure she was looking back at him, "your identity is not muddled. I think it's clearer than it's ever been. That's why it hurts." He tapped his chest. "And the pyrsi who can't accept that? You don't need them."

Dime sighed. She was so grateful for the two pyrsi that sat here with her. For her children, out in the complex. So grateful. But she didn't want to feel nervous stepping outside of that door every single turn, not knowing how someone would react. Keeping her heart open, a target at which they could toss their barbs.

"I don't fit in. I don't fit anyone's category of where a pyr should be. My scars—" She tapped one of her shoulders. "I know they're covered, but they're always here for me. I know they're always there. I know they prevent me from being exactly what anyone else wants me to be." She stared off at the wall. She wasn't saying it right, and she couldn't explain it. Maybe she should stop trying. Stop complaining. Get back to doing normal things and let the world figure itself out.

"They are part of you," Ador said. His tenor had changed, and he was quiet. Serious.

Dime wasn't sure what he meant.

"Your scars. I haven't had the same experiences as you, so I wouldn't presume to know how you feel, but you still talk about the scars as though they are foreign to you. They are part of you. Just as any hurt that's been done to you is part of you. It's part of who you are." He tapped his chest. "I have scars too. Two scars, not unlike your own." He traced a finger across the front of his shirt—first on one side, and then on the other. Dayn sat still beside him.

It took her a stride, and she realized Ador must be referring to the removal of breast tissue, done long ago. Dime knew that Ador had not always been identified as ma'pyr, but it wasn't something that she thought about. Nor had she known if he'd had any surgery, nor would she have asked. Pyrsi had different bodies. Some changed theirs. Others didn't. It was a pyrsonal matter, unless a pyr chose to share their journey.

"It's different," he said, interrupting her thoughts. "I was elated to get my surgery, while your body was changed without consent. My body grew in a form that caused me not to see myself in the mirror. I could sit back and resent the time it took me to understand that, or I could accept myself as who I am now. I can be proud of it. I am not just a ma'pyr, Dime. I'm a ma'pyr with scars."

Dime struggled for what to say.

"I'm sorry. Maybe this doesn't make sense." Ador wrung his hands together. "I just don't want to see you spend cycles not seeing yourself in the mirror, when this . . . this *is* you. All of it.

"I know it's easy to say, oh, just be who you already were before these events. But these events are now part of you. The knowledge of how someone else's past actions affect you now is part of you. Their valence is part of you. The pull of the culture, of the characteristics of your blood, they emerge within you. The *hurt* is in you. You can't ignore it more than any other part of yourself."

He rested a hand across his chest. "This is who I am. So, Dime who are you?"

"I don't know," she murmured. That was the problem. She wasn't sure.

"I do," Dayn said. "I know you. And yes, you're changing. But aren't we all? Shouldn't we all? Hey. We'll get through it together."

"Thanks." Dime felt she should have a more elegant response, but she was just so lucky to have a spouse and a friend like this. Yet there was something inside her now. Something new. Or awakened. A tiny light.

"I need to take a walk," she said, rising. "I'm fine. Just need to think."

The ma'pyrsi both nodded, their eyes following her.

As she walked to the side stand and poured a cup of water from the pitcher, she gazed back across the room. Dayn and Ador were resuming their game, the flyer still sitting between them on the table. She watched as they dealt cards overtop her face. With a tiny snort, she left, back into the hallway.

Instead of a more generic walk, Dime wandered off to find the shop where Tum was working. Not exactly sure how to get there, she cut through the dining hall, and was relieved when one of the servers, seeing her hovering tentatively by the wall, came over and told her where it was.

As she turned into the side corridor, she heard a voice behind her. "Dime?"

Dime turned to see a beautiful fairy, maybe closer to Ella's age, hurrying from the large room and out to where she waited. Instead of long and styled hair, xyrs was cut short and fell in wide curls, dyed a rich forest brown. She was taken by the pyr's broad smile.

"Yes, hello."

"I'm Fe'Trowby. I was at one of your sessions. I hadn't had the chance to meet you, but I wanted to say I enjoyed listening to your ideas."

"Oh, thank you, Trowby. It's so nice to meet you. I've . . . had a tough time." She didn't know why that last bit had rushed out, but the fairy just felt like someone who would care.

"I know," Trowby answered. "If I can help you with anything, please let me know."

"Well, sure," Dime thought about how to answer, and suddenly it was clear. She'd come here for a coalition and felt that she'd completely failed at that goal. Yet maybe this fe'pyr was that start. At the thought, she brightened a touch more. "We're gathering pyrsi who will help promote conversation instead of division. I'm leaving soon, but if you're interested, I would make sure you talk to one of the visitors, Fe'Volana, before she leaves too. She wears the ribbon dress." Trowby nodded, as if familiar. "She can get you connected with the Foundry. If . . . if you're willing to return to the forest for a while."

"That's where I always wanted to be," she answered, her voice quieting. "But pyrsi here, I've been able to help them too." Her smile lifted. "I'd love to join you. I will talk to Volana. Thank you. Safe travels—and don't hesitate to let me know if you need anything else."

Dime went to fan her fingers, then stopped. "I do have a question, actually, and I've been embarrassed to ask it."

Trowby shook her head, as though to say no question should be embarrassing.

"This gesture," Dime curled her fingers. "I know that it is a greeting, like our fanned fingers, but what does it mean exactly? And would it be appropriate for a soly to use it?" Dime knew some were uncomfortable that she called herself a soly, as some of the fairies saw her as one of their own. But, it wasn't her culture, at least not yet. She didn't want to misstep.

Trowby didn't seem bothered by the question or the distinction. Instead she raised her hand in the gesture, her fingers curling down on top of each other before sliding slightly to the side. "Like this," she said. "It is the comfort of Sha. The peace as well as the storms, and its endless, continuing nature. That we remember our place in it, and take that comfort." She paused. "It just means hello or goodbye, but there is more to it that we all understand, so I wanted to explain. And yes, anyone may use it. Sha encompasses us all."

Dime waved her fingers. With the explanation, she now understood it better. It wasn't just a curl, but a wave.

"Now you've got it," Trowby said. "And your gesture?"

Reaching out her fingers, Dime fanned them out, then allowed them to rise, just a little. "Also a greeting. My father said it was symbolic of Sol's rays." She paused, trying to remember if he'd given a longer explanation. He probably had. Dime felt guilty for not having listened more closely.

"It was nice to talk to you," Trowby said, fanning her fingers. "I'll see you out there." She grinned, pointing upward.

"Likewise." Dime did her best to wave her fingers again, trying to keep the comfort of Sha in her mind. Then, Trowby was gone.

Once Dime rounded the last turn, the loud hammering noises gave her a pretty good sense she was in the right place.

Pyrsi turned to look as she entered, and she offered back fanned fingers and a tentative hello. Tum was in the center of the room, struggling to keep her balance as she worked a heavy lathe that required the full force of both her small but muscular arms. Dime's heart lifted at the sight.

Tum grunted as Dime sat down next to her.

"Need help?"

"Nope!" Tum wrenched the metal around, finally pulling the piece of wood free. "It's a leg. See how fancy it is? I need to smooth it now." She pointed over at a crumpled piece of sandpaper.

The little bundle of grit reminded Dime of an athlete, ready to be put into the game. She chuckled. Was she? Was she ready to get back in the game?

"It's a chair, for the tables. We make them different ways," Tum said. "Fairies with wings either don't use chair backs, or they like ones that are skinnier. They can sit against a wide back, but then their wings are stuck out to the side. And pyrsi without wings like the chair backs we're used to. I had to tell them about pyrsi like me. I said pyrsi like me need a chair we can get into and move around in with our arms, and I like having it tilt back a little. And it still has to be the same height, so I can join the others. I mean, a different height. Anyway—"

As Tum showed no signs of stopping, Dime didn't interrupt. And Tum began sanding the petite chair leg, continuing to tell Dime about the tools she'd learned to use and the pyrsi she'd met.

Content for the first time in a while, Dime relaxed back and listened to the innocently happy voice of her beautiful child, now waving what looked like a chisel.

"Do you know Uchitar is a carpenter?"

Dime did not know that. "No. That's cool."

"I hope he's able to get better soon."

Dime hoped so too. There was a clear difference between using a substance and being controlled by one. And though she'd not discussed it with Uchitar himself, Volana had mentioned his desire to stop taking tzetz entirely. She'd also said he was visiting someone now, and her tone had indicated there was a long story there. Dime hoped he was doing well.

"Tum?" Dime finally decided to broach the subject, as Tum's own stories had trailed off.

"I know. You're going to leave again. I think you should, too. I'll miss you, though." There was a finality in Tum's words. A lack of desire to discuss, but a sense of what had to be done that reminded Dime of herself.

"Are you ok to stay here a while?" she asked instead. "Bown says there are teachers here who will continue your classes, and medics of both cultures with whom Luja can study."

Tum didn't look up. "I know. Da-da said he'd stay with us. He said there were some caves in the back that he wanted to study while we were here. But then he said that you and Volana and Ador and Hin have to go. But it's just for a while."

"I promise I'll see you soon." She hoped the idea that something could prevent her from that promise was implied, because she didn't want to say that. She knew Tum meant that she promised to do her best.

"Ma-ma?" Tum looked up, the chair leg in her hand. "Stop doubting yourself."

When Dime reached the platform where her chair again rested, instead of taking off, she sat down for a while. Though she'd had a quick sleep before leaving, here, she allowed herself just to rest. To watch the way that Sol's light fell against the circle of rocks and made intricate shadows across the rocky ground. To listen to the sound of rustling brush, scurrying beings, and flying birds. To feel her skin grow warm in the light.

Dime was tired of being a miniature in someone else's game.

And so, it was time to go. Time to figure this out. Time to either help guide Ada-ji to a state of progress or at least be present, doing her best, as the pieces fell. As she rose then lowered into her roughly-constructed seat, nothing like the refined touches of Tum's or Dayn's woodwork, something hard scraped against her leg.

Reaching down, there was a bump in Dime's right side-pocket, one that had snagged on the arm of the chair. As her hand dipped into the pocket, her fingers wrapped around an unquestionable shape. A rough octahedron, cool and smooth to the touch.

Pulling the chain out, the blue-hued diamond swayed from her gray fingers. Sol's light burst through it, projecting rainbows onto the tall rocks within which she'd rested the platform, back when they'd first arrived.

The effort it must have taken Zael, tired and breathless, to shove the stone back into her pocket was a clear enough sign that it was where it needed to be. For now. She twirled her fingers, allowing the rainbow beams to dance around her. Then, she closed her eyes, feeling them even more immensely in the depths of her own mind. In her heart.

Her respite here ended up not being so much of a respite. Maybe there was no respite sometimes when the wounds were still fresh. But there would be. She had to believe. And what had Zael said?

Dime clipped the diamond pendant back around her neck, and here, standing in Sol's warmth, she thought only of her friends.

No more stalling. No more detours. It was time to show this world who she was.

And to those who didn't try to understand that?

She owed them nothing.

END OF PART 06

ABOUT THE AUTHOR

E.D.E. Bell was born in the year of the fire dragon during a Cleveland blizzard. After a youth in the mitten, an MSE in Electrical Engineering from the University of Michigan, three wonderful children, and nearly two decades in Northern Virginia and Southwest Ohio developing technical intelligence strategy, she now applies her magic to the creation of genre-bending fantasy fiction in Ferndale, Michigan, where she is proud to be part of the Detroit arts community. A passionate vegan and enthusiastic denier of gender rules, she feels strongly about issues related to human equality and animal compassion. She revels in garlic. She loves cats and trees. You can follow her adventures at edebell.com.

Continue Dime's story in . . .

Part 07: Will

edebell.com/diamondsong